T0095697

Flying on Fabric

Marc A. Rossi

TRUE DIRECTIONS
AN AFFILIATE OF TARCHER PERIGEE

iUniverse®

FLYING ON FABRIC

iUniverse books may be ordered through booksellers or by contacting:

iUniverse
1663 Liberty Drive
Bloomington, IN 47403
www.iuniverse.com
1-800-Authors (1-800-288-4677)

Because of the dynamic nature of the Internet, any web addresses or links contained in this book may have changed since publication and may no longer be valid. The views expressed in this work are solely those of the author and do not necessarily reflect the views of the publisher, and the publisher hereby disclaims any responsibility for them.

Any people depicted in stock imagery provided by Thinkstock are models, and such images are being used for illustrative purposes only. Certain stock imagery © Thinkstock.

ISBN: 978-1-4917-9121-9 (sc)
ISBN: 978-1-4917-9122-6 (hc)
ISBN: 978-1-4917-9123-3 (e)

Library of Congress Control Number: 2016904217

Print information available on the last page.

iUniverse rev. date: 06/13/2017

Chapter 1

Ann dismounted her bike and crouched behind some bushes near the entrance of the little airfield located on the edge of town. The hot Florida sun bore down on her bare arms as she examined the area. There wasn't much to see. America had just entered the space age by shooting John Glenn into orbit a few months before in a Mercury space capsule, but this place looked more like something Orville and Wilbur Wright would have called home sixty years earlier. The airfield consisted of nothing more than an old run-down wooden hangar and a faded wind sock hung from a rusty pole at one end of a long grass runway. An old decrepit camper trailer was parked near the hangar, but Ann couldn't see any indication that it was actually occupied. All the windows were covered by sun-faded curtains, and weeds grew around the flattened tires. She spotted a sign that someone had stuck haphazardly alongside the bumpy gravel road leading to the entrance of the airfield. The faded, weathered paint on the sign simply said "Airfield," with an arrow pointing in the general direction of the hangar. It didn't look like much, but it was the only place to land an airplane within thirty miles of Indiantown.

Ann wasn't there to watch the comings and goings at the forlorn little airfield but instead had come to perform a rite of passage so that she would be accepted by the local boys into their gang. She had tried to make friends with the girls in the neighborhood, but they were into playing with dolls, gossiping, and avoiding getting dirty. Ann much preferred the mischief the boys wound up getting into as opposed to "girlie" things. Her mother called Ann a tomboy as if that were a bad thing, but Ann wore the label with pride. She could do anything the boys could do just as well as they could, if not better, and she never backed down from an opportunity to prove it to anyone who would give her the chance.

"Well, are you going to do it, or are you going to chicken out?" Billy Henderson nudged her shoulder.

Billy was the ringleader of the little gang that included Joey Reed and Tommy Johnson. Billy was a year older than Ann but had been held back, so they would actually be in the same grade when school started in the fall. Joey and Tommy went along with anything Billy told them to do. Ann guessed this was primarily because Billy was much bigger and stronger than the two other boys put together. Ann had heard that Billy was known for passing out more than a few black eyes among his schoolmates and probably spent as much time in detention as he did in class.

"I'm telling you the old man is crazy," Joey said. "My dad says it's from all the chemicals he's been spraying all these years. The chemicals have eaten his brain out from the inside, making him loopy."

"I heard it was from the war," said Tommy. "I heard he shot down a bunch of Jap planes and then crashed on a deserted island. He was there for years until they found him, and by then he had gone nuts."

Billy gave them both a look of annoyance. "You are both idiots." He spoke with an air of authority. "He's just a crazy old drunk that's going to kill himself one day flying into a tree or telephone pole. You've seen the way he flies that old crop-dusting crate."

Ann watched in disgust as Tommy and Joey just meekly nodded in agreement. She had been hanging out with the boys for only a week but already knew that Tommy and Joey would always fall in line with whatever Billy had to say. She had already made up her mind that she wasn't going to let Billy intimidate her like he did the others.

"I'm not chickening out!" Ann snapped back at Billy in a determined voice. "I don't care if the old man is crazy or not. It doesn't matter to me. I'll do it."

Ann really didn't know anything about the owner of the airfield other than his name. She had never even seen a crop-dusting plane before she moved with her mother to Indiantown from Baltimore at the beginning of summer. But just a few days before, she had witnessed a plane with two sets of wings roaring just inches above the ground and spewing a cloud behind it as she pedaled her bike along the road. Ann had watched as the plane popped over a tree at the very last second, avoiding disaster. Based on what she had seen, Ann was inclined to agree that whoever was flying the plane was crazy, regardless of what actually had brought on the condition.

Ann's mother had grown up in Indiantown. When Ann asked her about the plane, her mother had told her that it was owned and flown by a man everyone just called Jack. His family had owned a large amount of land on the outskirts of town generations before, but the estate had slowly been whittled down over the years until all that was left was the little airfield. Jack had been flying planes out of the airfield since before Ann's mother was born. He didn't come into town much, and when he did, he wasn't known for being social. He had a reputation for being a grumpy, cantankerous old man. Ann's mother told her that she was to stay away from Jack's place if she didn't want to get into trouble.

Ann watched as Billy peeked around the corner of the bushes to see if anyone was around. She positioned herself so she could see over Billy's shoulder and get a better view of the hangar. Everything was still in the morning air. The old faded wind sock hung limply on the pole at the far end of the runway. There appeared to be no movement at the hangar or the trailer.

"All right, Jack has an old beat-up pickup truck, and it's not here. He must be in town," Billy said, turning back to face Ann. "If you want to hang around with us, you have to prove yourself by sneaking into the hangar and stealing something. Come back empty-handed, and you are out for good."

Ann considered the challenge. The thought of stealing something from the hangar didn't raise a moral issue with her. It seemed every time she moved to a new place—and there had been a lot of moves since her mother and father's divorce—she had to pass some rite of initiation with the local kids in order to be considered one of the gang. Such initiations often involved petty theft, such as shoplifting a candy bar from a corner store, but stealing something out of the hangar of a crazy old crop duster seemed a different matter. She had no idea just how crazy this old man might be or what he would do if he caught her. Still, Ann never backed down from a challenge, even when she knew better, so she would go into the hangar and come back with something just to show the boys they were no better than her.

"What does it have to be?" Ann asked.

"Anything," Billy replied. "A tool, a can of oil, a spark plug, anything— just get in there and bring something back. You better not rat on us if you get caught, or I'll give you a black eye, even if you are a girl."

"If I get caught, it will only be because you are making too much noise, flapping that big mouth of yours. Be quiet for a change, or you'll get us all caught," Ann said sharply.

Billy was taken aback by her snapping at him. No one had ever said anything like that to him before, let alone a girl. Tommy and Joey started snickering at Ann's reply to Billy, until Billy glared at them and raised a fist. They knew the look, and it wiped the smiles from their faces.

"Do you two find something funny?" Billy growled.

Ann watched as Tommy and Joey just stared at the ground.

Receiving no reply, Billy turned his attention back to Ann and the task at hand. "Quit stalling and move!" Billy said as he grabbed Ann by the arm and pushed her toward the hangar.

Ann slapped his hand away and glared at Billy. "Don't touch me! I'll go when I'm ready."

Ann paused for a moment, just to make a point, before moving from the bushes to the side of the hangar to survey the scene. No one was around. She could see a rusty padlock hanging unused beside the side door and guessed that the door must have been left unlocked. She crept up to the side door and opened it a few inches to peek inside. It was dark and quiet inside the hangar. Hesitating for a moment, she looked back at the boys. She could see in Billy's beady little eyes and by the smirk on his face that he was daring her to go inside. Ann glared right back at Billy with all the confidence she could muster, opened the door, and slipped inside the hangar. She closed the door behind her, thankful that the rusty old hinges didn't squeak.

***

The hangar smelled old and dank. It reminded Ann of the musty wood aroma of an old barn mixed with the smell of grease and gasoline. Shafts of light came in at different angles from small openings between the boards of the hangar walls. A few small dirty windows at the back of the hangar allowed filtered bits of sunlight to pass through, providing the only available lighting. It took a few moments for Ann's eyes to adjust to the semidarkness. Once they did, she saw the crop-dusting plane she had seen flying low over the ground sitting directly in front of her. A smaller yellow plane with a single high set of wings sat beside the crop-dusting plane. In the far corner, surrounded by boxes and crates, there appeared to be another plane, abandoned and covered with dusty tarps.

Ann was momentarily startled by a mouse running along the base of the wall. She watched as it vanished under a door at the right back corner of the room. A metal cabinet sat against the side wall of the room and the rear hangar wall. A refrigerator was located next to the cabinet, along with a sink. A workbench ran along the rest of the back wall of the hangar to the far corner behind the tarp-covered plane.

Ann made her way over to the workbench. Several tools where haphazardly laid out. She picked up a few of the tools and examined them in detail. They were old but appeared to have been recently used since they were clean and free of rust. She had never seen some of the tools before and had no idea of their purpose. She then noticed an old screwdriver in the back, seemingly forgotten. It looked like something she could take without anyone noticing it was gone. Ann picked up the screwdriver and ran her finger along the shaft and blade, which were covered with a coat of rust from lack of use and care. *Clearly, this is something that won't be missed*, Ann thought.

***

The boys awaited Ann's return back at the bushes. It was taking longer than they wanted, and they were all beginning to get nervous. They knew Jack could show up at any time, and none of them wanted to be around when that happened. The last thing they wanted was another run-in with the crazy old guy.

"Do you think she'll really do it?" Tommy asked. "None of us has ever done it."

"You just keep your big mouth shut," Billy hissed at Tommy. "No one better tell her, or I'll pound them."

Joey whispered back, "We should get out of here. She's taking too long, and you know what he'll do if he catches us hanging around again. I'm in enough trouble with my father from the last time we tried to get into the hangar."

The boys were concentrating so hard on the hangar that they didn't bother to check behind them. Suddenly, the sun was blocked out by the shadow of someone looming over them. The boys all turned and looked over their shoulders in unison.

Jack towered over the boys with his hands on his hips. "I told you delinquents not to hang around here. Get out!"

The boys scrambled to get away, bumping into one another as they went. They jumped on their bikes and sped down the gravel road, almost crashing into one another as they raced away as fast as their legs could pump the pedals. Only Ann's bike remained behind where she had left it, partially obscured by the bushes.

***

Although Ann already had the screwdriver in her hand and had accomplished her goal, she had allowed her curiosity to get the better of her. Instead of heading for the door, she had turned her attention to the airplane that was covered by the dusty tarps at the far end of the hangar. She had to see what was under those tarps. Ann was just about to lift one of the tarps when she heard the commotion outside. She immediately bolted for the side door and was just a few steps short of reaching it when she heard the sound of the padlock being latched.

Ann began to panic as she looked for another way out. The whole front side of the hangar consisted of huge sliding doors that could be opened to roll out the airplanes. Ann turned and ran to the front of the hangar, but the sliding doors were locked from the inside with another padlock. She looked to the windows, but they were covered with bars. There was no way out. She was trapped.

Ann closed her eyes, trying to regain her composure. *Relax,* she thought. *Take a deep breath and think!* Maybe she could find a tool that could be used to break the lock on the main hangar doors. She opened her eyes, trying to readjust to the dim light. A groan escaped from her lips. She'd be grounded for eternity this time, particularly since her mother had specifically told her to stay away from Jack's. She had to get out of the hangar fast!

***

Jack walked back toward the road, passing the bushes where the boys had hidden. He had chased the same three boys away from the hangar not more than a few weeks ago. Jack wouldn't have been able to surprise them this time if he hadn't had to leave his truck in town and walk back because of a cracked distributor cap. They could always hear his old truck coming a mile away. It seemed to Jack that every year there was a new crop of juvenile delinquents trying to steal things from his hangar. Harassing him had apparently become a local rite of passage over the years, but he was certainly getting too old and tired to be dealing with these kids anymore.

He could still see the dust being kicked up from the fleeing pint-sized felons a hundred yards away as he looked down the road. It was then that he noticed another bike protruding from under the bushes. The boys must have added a fourth member to their gang. He looked around but couldn't find any signs of the owner of the bike. With a growing sense of satisfaction, he realized the new member of the group must be locked inside the hangar. He had one trapped like a rat! He was determined to haul the trapped delinquent before the police to teach the rest of them a lesson. Jack returned to the side door, unlocked it, and flung it wide open.

"I got you this time!" Jack yelled. "You are going to jail."

***

Sunlight streamed through the door, illuminating the inside of the hangar. Ann was startled and temporarily blinded by the light. Attempting to get out of the hangar as quickly as possible, she ran toward the door but stumbled into the crop-dusting plane and lost her balance. Her instincts took over, and she stuck out her hand in an attempt to break her fall. It was too late. Ann heard a horrible ripping sound as she hit the floor.

Ann stood up and stared in disbelief, first at a large gaping hole in the wing of the crop-dusting plane and then at the screwdriver still clutched in her hand. She had accidently plunged the screwdriver into the wing, tearing a large gash in it as she fell to the floor. She'd had no idea that the wing was covered in fabric instead of metal and couldn't believe a screwdriver could do that much damage to an airplane.

Looking up, she could see a man framed by the light of the door, but she couldn't make out his face. It must be Jack, she figured, but it really didn't matter. Whoever it was, she was quite sure his appearance was going to mean big trouble for her. She could hear the anger in his voice, and the word "jail" had rung in her ears. She would never be able to explain this one to her mother. She needed to get out of the hangar as fast as possible.

"Look at what you've done!" shouted Jack.

"I didn't mean to. It was an accident," Ann said in a trembling voice.

Jack shouted again, "Accident? Is it an accident you're in my hangar?"

Ann, regaining some composure, replied defiantly, "Well, who's stupid enough to have an airplane made out of cloth?"

The man appeared to be startled by her reply and hesitated for a moment before shouting in anger, "Why, you little ..."

Ann didn't wait to hear the rest of the sentence. As Jack moved forward to grab her, she ducked under his arm and scooted out the open side door, running as fast as her legs would carry her. She grabbed her bike and jumped on in a running stride. Not bothering to look behind her, she raced down the gravel road to the main street into town, peddling as hard as she could. Turning off on her street, she continued as fast as she could toward her own house, passing Billy's house along the way.

***

Billy, Tommy, and Joey were sitting on Billy's front porch, replaying their escape from Jack to some of the other neighborhood boys. As usual, Billy was doing all the talking, with Tommy and Joey nodding in agreement. The story, and Billy's role in it, grew bolder and grander with each retelling. Just as Billy had the boys spellbound with tales of his courage, Joey spotted Ann flying down the street on her bike.

"Hey, look!" Joey shouted, pointing to the street. "It's her!"

Ann didn't even bother to look their way but instead flung the screwdriver in their direction as hard as she could. The boys watched, transfixed, as the screwdriver tumbled end over end through the air until it stuck in the grass not more than a foot from Billy's feet.

"She did it, Billy. I can't believe it. She did it," Tommy said in awe.

Mouth hanging open, Billy was speechless for the first time either Tommy or Joey could remember.

Chapter 2

Bang! The sound of the front screen door banging shut and Ann's feet pounding up the stairs got her mother's attention. "Ann, I've told you a hundred times not to let the door slam. Now get washed up and come down for dinner. I've been waiting for you."

Even with her bedroom door closed, Ann could hear her mother, Sarah, scolding her from the bottom of the steps. It had become a ritual in the house. Ann would fly into the house every day, flinging the old wooden screen door open as far as the spring would allow and then letting it fly shut with a resounding bang against the jamb. Her mother would scold her about letting the door slam shut each time, but this never had much impact on her. It wasn't like Ann was even doing it intentionally—she wasn't making a conscious decision to let the door slam, but she also made no conscious effort to prevent it from banging shut.

Ann walked into the kitchen just as her mother was putting dinner on the table. She hadn't had any lunch and was starving after all the excitement of the afternoon. Ann sat down and eagerly reached for a basket of fresh biscuits her mother had just set down in front of her.

"Did you wash your hands?" her mother asked in a suspicious voice.

Ann didn't bother to reply other than to issue a noticeable sigh. She got up from the table and went to the kitchen sink. It seemed all her mother cared about was whether she had washed her hands, whether her hair was combed, and whether her clothes got dirty. Ann thought her mother would prefer to have a china doll that sat still all day and never got dirty rather than a child who liked to wander the outdoors.

"What were you up to this afternoon? I saw you go off with those neighborhood boys," said Ann's mother. "You weren't getting into trouble again, were you?"

"No. We were just riding bikes," Ann said, trying to reply in a matter-of-fact tone.

"Then why do you have that guilty look on your face?" said Ann's mother.

Ann wondered whether her mother was some sort of mind reader and should be working in a carnival sideshow reading palms for a living. Ann was a lousy liar and an even worse actress when it came to pulling the wool over her mother's eyes. Although Ann could fool others, it usually didn't take her mother long to deduce that Ann had been up to some form of mischief. The fact that Ann had been out all afternoon with Billy and his gang likely only reinforced her mom's suspicions. Still, Ann wasn't about to give in easily, even though she knew the battle was ultimately hopeless.

"What look?" Ann asked with all the angelic innocence she could muster.

"Ann, we haven't even been in town a month," her mother said. "Please tell me you aren't getting into trouble already."

"Why do you always assume I'm up to no good?" Ann replied defiantly, even though she knew her mother was right.

"Please, Ann, haven't we been through enough the last few years? I want you to stay away from those boys. They are only going to get you in trouble. Mrs. Johnson told me Billy Henderson spends more time in detention than he does in class. Why don't you make friends with some of the neighborhood girls? You have to make an effort to fit in here. We both have to make the best of the situation," her mother said with a pained expression on her face.

Ann knew that the distress her mother felt was real. As a teenager, Ann's mother had taken up with the local high school football hero against her parents' wishes and ended up pregnant with Ann at the age of seventeen.

As a result, she had never finished high school, and her parents had sent her out of town to live with an aunt during her pregnancy. Although Ann's father had eventually married her mother, it was a difficult relationship, and he ended up leaving when Ann was eight years old.

At first Ann had blamed her mother for her father leaving, and any attempts Sarah made to make Ann study hard, finish school, and not end up in a similar situation had only made Ann more rebellious. Recently, however, Ann had begun to feel that maybe her mother's pain was her fault. If she hadn't come along when she did, her mother would have had a much easier and happier life. Maybe her mother could have pursued her own dreams instead of working at low-wage jobs to support Ann.

Ann's grandmother had recently passed away and left the house in Indiantown and a little money to Ann's mother. Ann knew it had been difficult for her mother to even consider coming back to the town where she had faced disgrace, but they didn't have any other viable options after the factory her mother worked at closed down in Baltimore. They were able to get by now with the little money her grandmother had left and with Ann's mother working two part-time jobs, but it wasn't easy to make ends meet. Ann began to feel guilty at the thought of what her mother had given up to raise her.

"I know … I know," Ann said.

"Now sit down and eat."

Ann pushed her food around the plate for a minute. "Mom, you know the old man who flies the crop-dusting plane around here?"

"Who, Jack? I already told you to stay away from him. Why?"

Ann continued to push her food around her plate. "Is he crazy?" she asked.

"Crazy? Jack? Who told you that? No, I don't think he's crazy. He isn't the nicest person in the world. It seems like he is always grumpy and complaining. He's a bit of a recluse. I remember he was always yelling at us kids to stay off his property when I was young."

Ann frowned.

"*Ann*," her mother said, drawing out her name, "have you been messing around Jack's place?"

The doorbell rang before Ann had a chance to respond. Her mother got up and went to the door as Ann continued to push the food around her plate and take occasional nibbles. Ann didn't give much thought to who might be at the door until she heard a man's voice mention her name. She leaned back in her chair as far as she could in an attempt to eavesdrop and get a glimpse of the person standing at the door.

***

"Hello, Sarah. It's been a long time. I don't think I've seen you since high school. I heard you moved back to town after your mom passed," the officer said sympathetically.

"Hello, Aubrey. I didn't know you were a police officer."

"Well, actually, I'm the police captain. I'm going on five years now on the job—although I have to admit, I'm also the whole department since we had to lay off Tom Jenkins last year. Anyway, it's good to see you back in town, Sarah."

Jack stood right behind Aubrey and had a look on his face that made it clear that all was not right with the world.

"It's good to see you again, Aubrey, but I take it this isn't a social visit?" Sarah said, eyeing Jack.

Jack answered before Aubrey had a chance to respond. "No, this ain't no social visit!" he shouted.

"I'm afraid not. Sarah, you know Jack, don't you?" asked Aubrey.

"Of course, I know Jack. Everyone in town knows him," Sarah replied in the most pleasant voice she could muster under the circumstances. "How are you doing, Jack?"

Sarah's polite greeting did nothing to soothe the anger on Jack's face.

Aubrey continued, "I'm afraid Jack wants to register a complaint against your daughter."

"Ann? Why? What has she done?"

"I'll tell you what your little juvenile delinquent has done. She's stolen from me. She took something from my hangar. Those little crooks are always stealing things from me!" Jack shouted.

13

"How do you know it was Ann?" Sarah asked.

"I recognized her bicycle out in the front yard on the way back to fix my truck. That's her bike, isn't it?" Jack pointed out toward the bike lying in the front yard.

"Yes, that's Ann's bike, but if Ann did take something from you, I'm sure she will be willing to apologize and give it back," said Sarah.

"Yeah, and who's going to pay for the repair of my airplane and for my lost wages?" asked Jack.

Aubrey stepped in to try to cool the situation down before Jack got even more agitated. "You see, Sarah, I'm afraid it's a little more serious than the usual prank. It seems your daughter put a tear in the wing of Jack's airplane. He'll have to repair it, and he may lose some work while the plane is down."

Sarah had a sinking feeling in her stomach. She had no extra money to pay for repairs to Jack's plane or to compensate him for his lost time. "Ann!" Sarah turned her head toward the kitchen. "You get over here right now!"

Ann approached the adults at the front door with her head down, dragging her feet all the way.

"Ann, is it true? Did you steal something from Jack's hangar?"

Ann couldn't meet her mother's eyes. She stood quietly staring at her shoes.

"Ann, answer me!"

"Yes, I took an old rusty screwdriver." She worked up the courage to meet her mother's agitated stare. "It's no good to anyone anyway."

"That's no excuse for stealing. Did you damage Jack's plane?"

"That was an accident!" Ann cried out.

"Accident or not, this little delinquent damaged my property." Jack pointed a long bony finger at Ann. "I want her prosecuted."

"Now, Jack, I'm sure you don't want me hauling this young lady off to the county juvenile detention hall." Aubrey offered a smile to Jack.

Jack's face brightened noticeably not in response to Aubrey's smile but at his mention of juvenile detention. "That's *exactly* what I want," Jack retorted as he poked Aubrey in the chest.

"What if she apologized and paid you back?" Aubrey said, trying to pacify the old man.

Jack remained stubbornly fixed in his position. "I don't want paid back. I want her prosecuted! I want her punished. These delinquents need to be taught a lesson so they will stop pestering me once and for all."

"I don't think I can pay much in damages," Sarah said, shaking her head. "I'm barely making ends meet."

"See! Arrest the little truant now!"

Aubrey sighed. "Just cool down, Jack. What if Ann worked off the debt?"

"Worked off the debt doing what? I don't need a snot-nosed kid running around my property and getting in my way."

"Well, she can help you clean up that hangar of yours," Aubrey replied.

Jack and Ann protested at the same time. "There's nothing wrong with my hangar."

"I'm not cleaning up that place," Ann exclaimed over Jack. "It's a mess and full of mouse poop!"

"Ann, you'll do what I tell you," Sarah said, giving her daughter a narrow stare before turning to Jack. "If you let Ann work for you, I'll make sure she shows up and does whatever you want. I don't have much, but I can probably pay for the materials to patch your plane."

"You don't get it, lady. I don't want your kid working for me. I want her in jail. I want her taught a lesson she won't soon forget!"

"Well, Jack, I can see your point," Aubrey said. "I guess I could just arrest this young lady and charge her with destruction of private property."

A smile of satisfaction crossed Jack's face.

"By the way, Jack, isn't that hangar of yours due for a fire inspection?" Aubrey asked.

The smile on Jack's face disappeared quickly. "What fire inspection? What are you talking about?"

"In addition to police chief, Sarah, I also happen to be the fire chief of the local volunteer fire department. I believe there is a county regulation requiring all businesses to have an annual fire safety inspection."

A look of consternation spread across Jack's face. "Now wait a minute. I see where you are going. You are trying to blackmail me."

"Blackmail?" Aubrey shrugged. "I don't know what you are talking about."

"I don't want to be anywhere around that old goat," Ann said, meeting the old man's contemptuous stare with one of her own.

"You'll do what I say, or I will let Aubrey arrest you and haul you off to the county jail." Sarah shot her daughter a look that caused Ann's bravado to wither.

"Okay then, it's all settled. Ann will apologize to Jack and work for him until the debt is paid off. I'm sure I've got better things to do than inspect your hangar, Jack."

"Blackmail!" Jack grumbled to himself.

"I'd rather go to jail!" Ann cried out.

"Do we have a deal or not?" Aubrey looked from Jack to Ann.

Ann threw her hands in the air and pounded up the stairs, grumbling all the way. Her footsteps echoed through the house as she slammed her bedroom door.

Jack scoffed and cursed under his breath. He swung the screen door wide as he went back out to his truck, stretching the spring to its maximum extension. Aubrey and Sarah cringed at the same time when the door slammed closed.

Aubrey looked to Sarah. "I guess that's a deal."

"Thanks, Aubrey. I've been having a hard time with her since her father left."

"That's okay. I remember another rather rambunctious young lady, and she seems to have turned out just fine." Aubrey winked at Sarah and went on his way.

Chapter 3

S   arah thought she was dreaming, but the incessant telephone
          ringing continued no matter how hard she tried to block it out.
          She forced her eyelids to open and saw the bright white numbers
of her bedside clock: 5:35 a.m.

A groan escaped her lips as she stumbled out of bed and made her
way downstairs. Her bare feet shuffled against the laminate floor of the
kitchen where the phone hung on the wall. "Hello?" She rubbed her sleep-
filled eyes.

"Where's that delinquent of yours?"

"What ... who is this?" Sarah replied groggily.

"It's Jack. Who else would it be? Tell your kid to get her behind over
here, or the deal's off, and I'll have her thrown in jail. She's already late."

"Jack?" She ran a hand through her disheveled hair. "It's only five
thirty in the morning."

"It's five thirty-five, and she's late. Is that what you teach your kid to
do—lie around all day in bed?" Jack's scratchy voice echoed through the
phone.

Sarah heard a click on the line before she could get in another word.
Sighing, she hung up the phone and made her way to Ann's bedroom. She
turned on the lights in Ann's room and began to shake her.

"Ann. You have to get up and get to Jack's right away."

Ann groaned and rolled over, pulling the covers over her head as she tried to ignore her mother.

Sarah grabbed the covers and pulled them off the bed. "Ann, get out of that bed right now!"

"What?" Ann whined.

"You have to get to Jack's. Hurry up—get going."

Ann groaned and looked out her bedroom window. Sarah followed her gaze. Only darkness was visible through the glass.

"It's not even light yet," Ann moaned.

Sarah shrugged. "Well, it's your own fault. If you had stayed out of trouble, you wouldn't have to be getting up so early. He's your boss now until you work off your debt. When you get done at Jack's, you come right home. I'm also grounding you for a month. I don't want you going off with those neighborhood boys and getting into more trouble."

"Grounded? That's not fair! I have to work for that crazy old man. Isn't that enough?"

"No, it isn't. I've taught you better than to steal from someone. Now get going," Sarah replied in a stern voice.

"But—"

"No excuses. You made your bed, and now you are going to have to sleep in it."

***

As her mother left her bedroom, Ann slowly swung her legs over the edge of the bed. It seemed to her that adults were always using some corny expression to reinforce their point. Grumbling under her breath about the unfairness of life, she reached down and grabbed a crumpled T-shirt and pair of jeans from the floor, where she had left them the night before. She pulled them on with her eyes still half-closed and dragged herself downstairs and toward the kitchen. Ann picked up an apple from a ceramic bowl on the table, wedged it between her teeth, and pushed open the front screen door, letting it slam behind her in the usual manner.

Her bike lay on the front lawn where she had dropped it after coming back from Jack's the day before. She grabbed the handlebars, stood the bike up, and began to swing her leg over the bike but then stopped herself. Instead of riding, she began walking the bike down the street at a leisurely pace. She decided that Jack could wait a few more minutes. In no rush, she played a game of connecting the dots between the circles of light cast on the ground from the few working streetlights. All the neighborhood homes she passed were dark except for the occasional lit porch light or lamppost that helped illuminate the way.

After passing the last streetlight and turning onto the dirt road leading to the hangar, Ann turned on the flashlight she had taped onto the handlebars to act as a headlight. Instead of picking up the pace, she walked even slower, taking a bite of the apple every now and then along the way. By the time she reached the old hangar, the sun had begun to yawn over the horizon, casting the beginning shades of yellow into the sky. She took the apple core and threw it with all her might into the sugarcane field across the road. Ann stood and watched for a moment as the apple core arched over the tall rows of cane and disappeared from her view. She could throw as well as any boy, but they still wouldn't let her play Little League, just because she was a girl.

Ann leaned her bike against the side of the hangar and stepped inside through the same door that had led to her present predicament in the first place. Jack was bent intently over the lower wing of his crop duster and didn't notice her arrival. His hand moved with purpose in a rhythmic motion as he passed a needle back and forth through a cloth patch he was sewing over the torn portion of the wing. Silence filled the air as she stepped lightly across the hangar floor and leaned over his hunched shoulder.

"You are sewing the airplane?" Ann said in a questioning voice.

"Darn it! You made me stick my finger!" Jack yelled as he jumped to his feet.

Ann stumbled backward at the same time.

"You don't just sneak up on people." Jack's eyelids narrowed. He checked on his finger, where a small dollop of blood pooled on the surface of his wrinkled skin.

"I didn't sneak up on you. Maybe you just can't hear anymore," Ann said.

"What?" Jack growled.

"My point exactly," Ann said to herself under her breath.

Jack grabbed a dirty rag from his back pocket and pressed it against his finger to stop the flow of blood. "You took your fine time getting here, didn't you? The sun's been up for a while." Jack removed the rag from his finger to check the wound. "I would be dusting now except for you. Get a broom and start sweeping. That's what you're supposed to be doing, isn't it?"

Ann squeezed her fists, her fingernails digging into her palms, but she did as she was told. An old broom with the bristles almost worn off was propped up against the wall near the side door. She grabbed the broom and swept back and forth in a lackluster manner, letting out a deep sigh with every few swipes. Jack didn't seem to notice or care about her dramatic performance. He had resumed his position curled over the wing of his plane. Examining his stitching, he nodded to himself in satisfaction. He picked up a small can and began brushing something over the patch with a small paintbrush. Ann wondered what he was doing and decided to make her way over to the plane to get a better look. With each sweeping motion, she took a little step closer to the old man, until she was right behind him once again.

"What's that?"

As Jack jumped, a string of curses tumbled from his mouth. "I told you to stop sneaking up on me, you little delinquent."

"I didn't sneak up on you, and don't call me delinquent." She straightened her back. "My name is Ann. What should I call you? My mother said I'm to show respect to *old people* by not using their first names, but I don't know your last name, so what should I call you?" Ann made sure to put special emphasis on the words "old people."

"You don't need to know my last name, and I don't need your sarcasm. My friends call me Jack, but you call me sir."

"Friends—that's a laugh," Ann mumbled out loud to herself.

"What did you say?"

Ann snapped to attention, putting the broom handle over her shoulder like a rifle and raising her hand in a salute. "Nothing, sir!"

"Are you always so sassy? Your father needs to put you over his knee and give that bottom of yours a few good whacks."

"I don't have a father. He's dead," Ann said.

She never told anyone the truth about her father. He had promised her he would come back the day he left, but he never did, and she had never heard from him again. Every birthday and every Christmas, she hoped to at least get a card from him, but she was always disappointed by an empty mailbox. To cover for that fact that her father had abandoned her, Ann had developed an elaborate story of how he had been a hero in the Korean War, saving a whole company of men. She had read about such a man in *Life* magazine and had made sure to memorize all the details in case anyone tried to question her story. Sadly, she would rather think of her father as a gallant dead hero than face the reality of his being a living deadbeat dad.

Ann could see from the expression on Jack's face that her comment had hit a raw nerve. It was obvious that he wasn't comfortable talking with most people, let alone a young girl, and he didn't know how to recover after having put his foot in his mouth. After an uncomfortable moment of awkward silence, he cleared his throat and answered her original question.

"It's called dope, and if you get much closer and smell it, then you will turn into one." He gave her a sideways glance. "That is, if you aren't one already."

"I'm no dope." She tilted her chin. "I'm very smart."

"Yeah, that was real smart of you to hang around with the rest of the town delinquents and steal from me."

"It was just a rusty old screwdriver that you weren't even using anymore."

"Does it matter? Was it your screwdriver or mine?"

Ann shifted uncomfortably. "Well … I was just … It was just …"

"Just what?"

"I just wanted to fit in with the boys. They dared me to do it. I didn't think you would even miss it."

"So if they dared you to jump off a bridge, would you do it?" Jack questioned.

Ann rolled her eyes. There it was again—an adult using another corny saying to teach her a life lesson. Ann considered for a moment that jumping off a bridge to get away from the old goat might be preferable to spending her day with him. She was being forced to show up and work, but she didn't want to listen to this crazy old man's opinions, even if she knew he was right. She changed the topic of conversation, going back to her original subject. "What's the dope for?"

Jack frowned. "Don't you ever stop asking questions?"

"Not until you answer them."

Jack sighed. Ann could tell from his reaction that he had come to the realization that the sooner he answered her questions, the sooner he would be rid of her.

"This airplane has a frame that is covered with fabric." He tapped the fabric-covered wing as he spoke. "When the fabric is damaged or *intentionally* ripped, you can sew on a patch and coat it with dope."

Ann couldn't ignore Jack's clear insinuation that she had intentionally damaged his airplane. "I told you before that I didn't mean to damage your plane. It was just an accident," she replied as she stepped back and away.

"It was no accident you were in my hangar when you weren't supposed to be, was it?"

Ann didn't reply. She knew he was right, and she shouldn't have been in the hangar in the first place.

Jack continued, "Anyway, as I was saying, the dope is like glue and gets hard. That's all that really holds the plane up in the air—just some dope-covered fabric stretched over a wooden frame of the wing. I'll have to let this dry and put another coat on before it's ready to fly. You've cost me a few days' worth of work."

Jack surveyed his patch job. Apparently satisfied, he wiped his hands on a rag and went over to the old white refrigerator in the back of the hangar. He opened it, grabbed a half-full carton of eggs and a package of bacon, and set them on the workbench. A vise was bolted onto the workbench, and a burning torch was clamped tight in the vise. Jack picked up a welding glove from the workbench and put it on his left hand. He then picked up a pair of pliers and used them to grab a sheet of metal that was leaning up against the wall at the back of the workbench. Holding the sheet of metal over the open flame with his left hand, he deftly cracked an egg with his right hand and plopped it onto the hot sheet. He continued with additional eggs and then threw strips of bacon on the sheet.

The savory smell of the eggs and bacon cooking lofted into the air and made Ann's mouth water, but she was turned off by what Jack was using as a stove. "Ew, what are you doing?"

Ann watched as Jack clenched his jaw at the thought of having to answer what to him was an obvious question.

"What does it look like I'm doing? I'm making breakfast. Haven't you ever seen someone cook an egg before?"

"Not with a blowtorch. Why can't you cook on a stove like normal people?"

"Well, if you must know, the stove in the trailer is broken," Jack replied in an annoyed manner.

"Why don't you fix the stove?"

Jack just grumbled to himself and finished cooking his breakfast. He turned off the torch, picked up a fork, and began eating right off the metal sheet.

Ann frowned at the thought of Jack's cooking methods, but her stomach groaned in response to the tasty smell of the eggs and bacon. In the end, her stomach won out over her head. "I didn't even get a chance to eat breakfast this morning. All I had was an apple."

"Well, it's hardly my fault if you can't get up on time and get your own breakfast. I'm not here to feed you."

"Well, it is kind of hard to do any useful work on an empty stomach. My mama always says that breakfast is the most important meal of the day." She stood with the broomstick in her hand, challenging him with her eyes.

"I'm surprised your mother has a chance to say anything, considering you never shut up."

His rebuff didn't deter her. She stood firm.

Jack looked at her just staring at him. He sighed and shifted. "All right," he muttered. "There is a plate over there in the cabinet. Go get it."

With a slight smile on her face at the thought of her little victory, Ann went over to the tall cabinet next to the refrigerator and opened the door. Like everything else in the hangar, the cabinet was disorganized and filled with various junk. The left side of the cabinet had a bar for hanging clothes. Ann noticed what appeared to be an old uniform hanging from the bar, covered with a protective plastic bag. The right side of the cabinet had several shelves filled with various items. A few plates and old coffee cups were placed on a higher shelf just within Ann's reach. One of the cups held a few pieces of old silverware. Ann took one of the plates, a knife, and a fork and rinsed them off in the sink beside the refrigerator before walking over to Jack and presenting the plate. Jack scraped a small portion of his eggs onto the plate. She stared at the meager portion.

"Well?" Jack grunted.

"What about some bacon?" Ann motioned to the crispy slivers of bacon on the metal sheet.

Jack muttered a few choice words, but Ann just smiled as he tossed the smallest piece of bacon onto her plate. She remained still and nodded her head toward the pile. After a few more grunts, he tossed on two more pieces.

"You know something," Ann said with a mouth full of food, "everyone thinks you're crazy."

Jack shrugged. "I don't care what anyone thinks, kid."

"Are you?"

"Am I what?" He didn't bother looking up from his plate.

"Crazy. I've seen you fly. Anyone that flies like that must be crazy. And my name is Ann, not kid or delinquent."

"Has nothing to do with being crazy. That's skill. I've been flying my whole life."

"That must be a long time. How old are you anyway?"

"Why do you ask so many questions? Can't you just be quiet? How old are you?"

"I'm thirteen." She stuffed a strip of bacon in her mouth.

"A delinquent teenager, that's just what I need around here." Jack got up and went to the sink to rinse off the metal sheet. "I need to go into town. You keep sweeping. When you're done with that, you can collect all the oily rags and put them in that barrel over there. Don't touch anything else. Understand?"

Ann nodded. "Well, if you want me to do some useful sweeping, you need to get me a new broom," she said as she picked up the broom she had been using and pointed to the worn bristles.

Jack scoffed. "Sweep," he said as he made his way out of the hangar.

When she saw his truck drive away, Ann dropped the broom. The sun had painted the sky hues of yellow and pink, and it was too beautiful to be stuck inside an old dusty hangar. A long strip of grass served as the airfield's runway. Ann walked out the front hangar door and lay down in the middle of the runway, back against a cushion of soft grass blades, eyes pointed toward the sky. A jet airliner passed through the patches of clouds far above. The white contrails from its engines painted lines across the sky. Ann couldn't help but wish she were a passenger on the plane, traveling to some far away, exotic location.

Chapter 4

The warm sun felt good as Ann lay in the soft grass of the runway and watched the puffy clouds floating across the blue sky. It wasn't long before she drifted off to sleep. The loud roar of an airplane engine woke her from a deep sleep and brought her back to her senses. Ann opened her eyes to see an airplane screaming past no more than twenty-five feet above her. She could feel the blast from the prop wash hot on her face. She jumped up and looked down the runway just in time to see the airplane zoom upward and bank sharply to the left.

Ann retreated back to the safety of the hangar, running as fast as her legs would carry her. When she was in front of the open hangar door, she turned back toward the runway in time to see the plane passing parallel to the runway only a few hundred feet in the air. Ann's mouth dropped open when she realized the plane was upside-down! She could see the pilot waving to her from the open cockpit. Ann managed to wave back out of reflex while standing dumbfounded, looking at the upside-down airplane.

She continued to watch the plane as it rolled over to an upright position, made a wide banking turn, and lined up with the runway. The loud, roaring engine suddenly went quiet except for an occasional popping sound. For a moment Ann thought the engine had stopped, but then she realized the propeller was still turning. The pilot had simply cut the engine power to let the plane glide down for a landing. As the plane approached the runway, the nose rose higher, and the plane seemed to float along just inches above the grass in slow motion. After what seemed like an eternity, all three wheels kissed the grass at the same time, and the plane rolled past Ann, coming to a stop in the center of the runway. The pilot of the airplane gunned the engine and spun the plane around to point it toward the hangar.

Ann was mesmerized by the little ballet performed by the airplane. The spinning airplane reminded her of the pirouettes she had practiced in the free ballet classes her mother had made her attend the previous summer at her last school. A local ballet company had offered to provide free dance lessons to underprivileged girls. Her mother had insisted that she at least try to participate in a more ladylike activity. Free or not, she hated ballet and would have much preferred spending her time playing baseball with the boys.

As the plane rolled toward her, Ann took a few more steps back, until she had crossed the threshold of the hangar door. The plane wasn't moving in a straight line but instead was swinging back and forth, making turns as it moved toward the hangar. Ann couldn't help but think that the pilot must be drunk if he couldn't even keep the plane moving in a straight line. Clearly, that couldn't be the case, however, or he wouldn't have been able to fly in the manner she had just witnessed.

Once the plane was in front of the hangar, the pilot gunned the engine once again to spin the plane around to point back out toward the runway. Ann got a better look at the plane as it spun. It had two sets of wings and a big round engine in the front and appeared to be newer and in better condition than Jack's crop-dusting plane. The pilot cut the engine, and the propeller came to a jerking stop. Ann watched as the pilot lifted himself from the cockpit, swung his legs over the side of the airplane, and stepped onto the lower wing. He was dressed in a khaki flying suit and was wearing a cloth helmet and flying goggles. He jumped down to the ground and removed his helmet to reveal thick, wavy black hair. Ann got a lump in her throat as he turned toward her to reveal deep blue eyes and a broad smile with the whitest teeth she had ever seen. He looked like a dashing star out of a Hollywood movie.

"Hello, young lady. What's your name?"

Ann just stood there and stared without responding.

"My name is Bill, Wild Bill to my friends. What's the matter? Cat got your tongue?"

Ann came to her senses. "My name is Ann."

"Well, Miss Ann, I suggest you not lounge around in the middle of the runway in the future. It's a good thing I always do a flyby and check the runway before landing. Otherwise, I might have landed and run right over you."

Ann hadn't even considered that possibility when she had gone out and lain down in the soft grass. This was the first plane other than Jack's that she had seen land at the field. It just hadn't occurred to her that someone else would use the field.

"Yes, sir," was all that Ann could muster for the moment.

"So what are you doing here? Where's Jack?"

"He went into town. I'm working for him, cleaning things up around the hangar."

"You are working for him?" Bill eyed her suspiciously. "I've never known Jack to have anyone around here working for him, let alone a young girl."

"Well, I am," Ann replied defensively. "Are you a friend of his?"

"A friend? I would say more of an acquaintance. I'm not sure Jack has any real friends anymore. Anyway, he called me and asked if I had some aircraft primer handy. Seems some local kid damaged his airplane, and he has to patch and paint it."

Bill turned back to his plane and opened a small baggage compartment located behind the cockpit. He reached in and pulled out a small can and handed it to Ann along with a small box. "Here, give these to him when he gets back. There is a set of spark plugs in the box that I owe him. I'm sorry Jack's plane was damaged, but I guess I would have to thank that kid. Jack asked me to spray a few fields for him while his plane is down, and I can use the work."

Ann wished Bill would stop mentioning the damage done to Jack's plane. She didn't need to be constantly reminded of what she had done.

It was time to change the subject. "Why were you turning back and forth when you brought the plane over to the hangar?"

"I can't see straight out the front. That's pretty common in a tail dragger. So I have to do 'S' turns to see what's ahead of me."

"A tail dragger?" Ann asked.

"Yeah, a tail dragger. You see, it has two wheels up front and a small wheel at the tail. The plane sort of looks like the tail is dragging behind, doesn't it?"

Ann nodded in agreement.

"In fact, in some of the very early planes, they used a skid instead of a wheel in the back, so the tail actually was dragging on the ground. I suppose that's where the term tail dragger originated. Anyway, the nose of the airplane is high in the air when you are taxiing, and it blocks the pilot's forward view. Other planes have nose wheels instead of tail wheels. They are easier to fly, and the pilot can look over the nose and see where he's going."

"What do you mean by 'taxiing'?" Ann asked.

"Oh, that's just the phrase to describe when a plane is maneuvering on the ground, but I thought you would know all this since you work for Jack," Bill said with a sly smile.

Ann tried to defend her lack of knowledge. "Well, I just started. I don't know much about airplanes yet, but I'm learning. What kind of plane is this?"

"It's a Stearman like Jack's. It was used as a trainer in World War II and then converted to a crop-dusting plane by putting a hopper in place of the front cockpit and spray nozzles along the lower wing."

Ann nodded. She had seen the nozzles on the lower wings of Jack's plane. "How long have you known Jack?" she asked.

"Oh, a long time. Almost all my life. I grew up around here and was friends with his son Henry. Jack taught me how to fly when I was just fifteen years old. He's a great pilot, but more than a little cranky. I don't know how many times I got a whack on the back of the head during training with that little ruler of his when I didn't do something to his satisfaction."

"Jack has a son?" Ann asked.

"I'm sorry to say Henry was killed in World War II. He was a marine fighter pilot on Midway and flew a Brewster Buffalo and was shot down by a Japanese Zero."

"What's Midway, what's a Brewster Buffalo, and what's a Zero?" Ann's questions were rapid-fire.

"Midway is an island in the Pacific. The Japanese wanted to capture the island. We won the battle, and it changed the course of the war in the Pacific for us. Don't they teach you anything about history in school?"

Ann shrugged and blushed at her lack of knowledge. History wasn't one of her best subjects. It all just seemed like a bunch of names and dates she had to memorize.

Bill let out a sigh and continued with his explanation. "The Brewster Buffalo was a fighter plane we had when the war began. Unfortunately, it was totally outclassed by the Japanese Zero, which was one of the very best fighter planes in the world at the beginning of the war. You might as well be flying a coffin, trying to fight a Zero in a Buffalo. I'm sure Henry knew his chances weren't very good when he flew off on his last mission. Every single Buffalo flying out of Midway was shot down by the Japanese."

Bill paused and wiped the sweat from his brow. "Jack took it pretty hard when he lost Henry and has never been the same since. His wife died when Henry was young, so Jack raised Henry by himself and taught him how to fly. I think Jack blames himself to this day for Henry's death."

"Why?" Ann asked.

"He thinks by teaching him to fly, he sent him to his death. I knew Henry pretty well, though. He was just as stubborn as Jack and loved flying. If Jack hadn't taught him, he would have found someone else to do it, and there was no way you were going to keep him out of the war. He wanted to take after Jack from the time he was a young boy."

It had never really occurred to Ann that Jack could be a husband and a father. She just thought of him as a grumpy old man and couldn't imagine anyone actually loving him or wanting to be in his presence on a daily basis. "He wanted to take after Jack? What do you mean?"

"You didn't know that Jack was a fighter pilot in World War I? He transferred from the horse cavalry and volunteered to fly. He shot down four German planes in 1918. One of them was on the tail of Eddie Rickenbacker and was about to shoot him down."

Ann looked at Bill with a blank stare.

"Eddie Rickenbacker. You do know who Eddie Rickenbacker is, don't you?"

Ann just shook her head.

"Geez, they really *don't* teach you anything in school. He was America's ace of aces during World War I and shot down twenty-six German planes. Rickenbacker wouldn't have survived the war, though, if Jack hadn't shot that German off his tail. Jack would have been an ace too if he hadn't gotten into flying so late in the war."

"What do you have to do to become an ace?"

"Easy. Just shoot down five enemy planes. But most fighter pilots never even came close to becoming an ace, especially during World War I, when the average pilot lasted just hours in battle. Those early planes were really dangerous to fly, so if the pilots weren't killed by the enemy, they often died from airplane accidents before they even had a chance to make a real difference in the fight."

Ann was dumbfounded. Jack was a real war hero? She never would have guessed.

"What do you know about Jack?" Bill asked.

"Nothing really. I just moved here. My mom just told me he's been here a long time. She grew up here too."

"Really? What is her name?"

"Sarah Wilson. Well, her maiden name was Sarah Franklin."

"How about your father? Did he grow up here too?"

"My father is dead. He died in the Korean War saving a whole company of men single-handed. He was a hero." Ann left it at that and didn't bother giving Bill her father's first name. The last thing she wanted to discuss was her father.

"Well, I'm very sorry to hear about your father, Miss Ann." He paused for a moment before continuing. "Sarah Franklin. I think I know her. She's younger than me, but if I remember correctly, she was quite the tomboy and pretty cute. She gave my younger brother Tommy a black eye for trying to steal a kiss."

"My mother was a tomboy? I don't think you have the right person." Ann scoffed at the idea of her prim and proper mother fighting and giving a boy a black eye.

"Well, maybe I'll just have to stop by sometime and see for myself." Bill winked at Ann and flashed a big, broad smile at her. "Now don't forget to give Jack the can of primer and those plugs."

"No, sir."

"I said my friends call me Wild Bill." He smiled again at her. "By the way, you don't seem like much of a delinquent to me."

Ann's face turned red. Bill had known all the time that she was the one responsible for the damage to Jack's plane. He had been teasing her the whole time.

Bill was back in his plane before Ann could say another word. He yelled out, "Clear!" before starting the engine. It kicked to life, with white smoke billowing out of the exhaust pipes. The wind from the propeller blew Ann's hair back as Bill gunned the engine and taxied down to the far end of the runway, making S turns all the way. Bill turned the plane into the wind and applied full power. Ann watched as the plane rolled forward and lifted gracefully off the grass. After a few minutes, the drone of the engine faded away, and Ann was alone again, or at least she thought she was alone.

"Pssst. Hey. Over here."

The whisper from the side door caused Ann to turn. She saw Billy's head peeking around the door. Ann walked out the side door and confronted him. She noticed Joey and Tommy standing by the bushes, holding their bikes.

"We saw Bill fly off, and Jack's truck is sitting outside the hardware store. Are you alone?"

"Yeah, I'm alone. Why?"

"We heard you got caught, and they were going to throw you in jail."

Ann crossed her arms over her chest. "I didn't get caught, and I'm not going to jail. Where did you hear such a stupid thing?"

"Then what was Aubrey doing over at your house?" Billy said.

"Yeah!" Tommy and Joey simultaneously chimed in.

"He's an old friend of my mother and was just saying hello." Ann hoped they'd go away. She didn't want them to know that she was stuck working for Jack as punishment for getting caught.

"That's a lie!" Billy shouted. "We saw Jack's truck there too."

Ann fidgeted. She had already dug herself into a hole by starting the lie, so she might as well dig a little deeper. "Jack was talking to my mother. He's going to teach me how to fly," Ann replied.

"He is not. That old goat would never teach anyone to fly, let alone a girl," said Billy.

"Yeah," Tommy agreed. "Girls don't fly airplanes anyway."

"Well, this one does—or I will. I'll be flying before summer is over," Ann said in a determined voice.

"You are such a liar. You just remember what I said about ratting us out. You say one word about us being out here with you, and I'll pound you. You won't be able to hide. Come on, guys. Let's leave the jailbird to her chores."

The boys jumped on their bikes and started pedaling down the road. Ann ran after them, yelling as loud as she could, "I will too fly! You just wait and see. I will!"

Ann wasn't about to back down at this point. She had no idea how she was going to do it, but she was going to find a way to get Jack to teach her to fly. She would show these boys she could do anything that a boy could do.

Chapter 5

Ann was now determined to convince Jack to teach her how to fly, which meant she would have to find a way to get on his good side. The only problem was she wasn't sure whether Jack had a good side. She immediately set to work with a sense of purpose. Instead of moving the broom back and forth in a lackluster manner, she put all the force she could into it, in order to eke out the last bit of usefulness from the already-worn broom bristles. After sweeping the dirt off the hangar floor and out the door the best she could, she proceeded to pick up all the oily rags she could find scattered about the hangar and put them in the barrel as instructed by Jack. Then she washed her breakfast plate and fork but couldn't find a clean rag or towel to dry them. Instead, she placed the fork on the plate and left them out to air-dry on the workbench.

Jack still hadn't returned by the time she was done. Remembering his admonishment not to touch anything, Ann concluded that this didn't mean she couldn't look around. She started by opening the door in the back corner of the hangar under which she had seen the mouse disappear. She expected to find a closet, but the room was actually a bathroom filled with various boxes in a haphazard manner.

Next, she opened the door of the cabinet and took a closer look at the hanging uniform that was preserved in a plastic bag. She didn't know much about the military, but she'd seen a few recruiting posters. The uniform looked like it was from the marines. She concluded that it was probably Henry's.

Ann continued to survey the contents of the cabinet until a wooden box on the very top shelf caught her attention. It was different from the rest of the items stashed on the lower shelves. The box sat alone, as if in a place of honor. Ann's curiosity got the better of her. She pulled over a wooden stool from its place in front of the workbench and climbed on top. Careful not to disturb anything else, she reached up to the top shelf and took down the box.

She opened the lid to reveal a small framed picture sitting atop the rest of the contents. The picture showed two men standing beside a plane parked in front of the open hangar. The older man was clearly Jack in his younger days. Next to him stood an even younger man, no older than eighteen or nineteen, with different features but the same resolved look in his eyes that she had seen in Jack's. This had to be Jack's son Henry. Ann didn't recognize the plane. It clearly wasn't the same one that Jack used for crop dusting. The plane in the picture had a cover over the engine, whereas the engine on Jack's plane was uncovered. Ann looked past the plane and the men at the hangar itself. It looked neat and orderly in the picture, in far contrast to the current state of affairs.

Ann found several small cases under the photograph that reminded her of jewelry boxes, along with a watch and a ring. She opened one of the boxes to reveal a military medal neatly pinned to the inside. The watch was old and had a cracked crystal. She noticed that the ring appeared to be a high school class ring and had the year 1939 stamped on the side. Ann reasoned that these things, like the uniform, had to have belonged to Henry.

Just then she heard the sound of Jack's truck coming down the road. She returned the contents to the box exactly as she had found them, closed the box, and carefully placed it back in its position on the top shelf before climbing off the stool and replacing it in front of the workbench. The door of Jack's truck slammed. He would be through the door in a few seconds. Ann picked up the plate and fork and hurried back over to the cabinet just as Jack came through the side door of the hangar.

"What are you doing?" Jack eyed her with suspicion.

"Nothing. I'm just putting the plate and fork back," Ann said as she reached up and placed them back in their original location.

Jack grunted and looked around the hangar. Nothing seemed out of place.

"I swept the floor best I could and picked up all the rags like you told me."

"Really?" Jack said, as if he hadn't expected her to do anything while he was gone.

"Yes, sir," Ann replied in a respectful manner. "What else would you like me to do?"

Jack noticed Ann's demeanor had changed completely between the time he had left and the time he returned.

"Oh, before I forget, Wild Bill dropped by and left you a can of primer and a box of spark plugs. I put them over on the workbench for you."

"Wild Bill." Jack snorted to himself at the thought of a grown man going around calling himself by a stupid nickname.

"Yes, sir. He said you taught him how to fly."

"You wouldn't know it by the way he buzzes around and shows off."

"Well, I don't know. It seemed like he really knew how to handle his plane. He was flying upside down!"

"Let me tell you something, kid. There is an old saying in aviation. There are old pilots, and there are bold pilots, but there aren't any old bold pilots. Bill is a bold pilot, and if he doesn't change his ways, he'll never get to be an old pilot."

Ann thought about how to steer the conversation away from Wild Bill and back toward her ultimate goal of asking Jack to teach her to fly. "Well, anyway, have you taught many people to fly?"

"More than a few and less than a lot, I suppose, but I don't do that anymore. My teaching days are over," Jack said in a distracted manner as he picked up the can of primer and examined the label.

"Did you ever teach a girl to fly?" Ann asked innocently.

Ann could tell Jack wasn't fooled by the offhand way she had asked the question. She sensed that he knew the real point of her inquiry.

"Can't say that I ever did, and I never will," Jack replied.

"Why? Is it because you think girls can't fly?" Ann demanded.

"Of course not. Haven't you ever heard of Amelia Earhart?"

This time the name was familiar to Ann, but she couldn't quite remember why. "Of course, I've heard of Amelia Earhart," she said, bluffing.

"Sure you have," Jack said skeptically. "She was the first woman to fly across the Atlantic, but they wouldn't let her actually fly the plane. She had to go as a passenger. So she got herself her own plane and flew it solo across the Atlantic."

"Like Charles Lindbergh!" Ann blurted out. They had talked about Charles Lindbergh in school the year before. He had flown from New York to Paris to win a prize. Ann wasn't a big fan of history, but Lindbergh's story had caught her attention because he was considered an underdog. Other people had more money and bigger airplanes, but Lindbergh was able to do it flying by himself in a tiny plane called the Spirit of St. Louis. If nothing else, Ann loved an underdog.

"That's right. Lindbergh was the first to fly the Atlantic and did it by himself. He was just an unknown airmail pilot before that flight. Earhart was the first woman to make the crossing in an airplane and also the first woman to fly the crossing solo. Well, at least you know about Lindbergh." Jack grumbled the last comment under his breath, but Ann heard it clearly.

Ann couldn't help but smile. It was the first nice thing that Jack had actually said to her, even if it was in an offhand sort of way. "So why won't you ever teach a girl to fly?" Ann persisted.

"Because I never did before, and I'm through with teaching anyone to fly. I don't care if it is a man, woman, or girl!"

Ann decided that the best course of action would be to drop the subject for the moment. She wasn't about to give up, but she knew better than to push the point. "So what else would you like me to do? How about I clean out that closet?" Ann said, pointing to the bathroom door and not letting on that she knew what the room was.

"That's a bathroom, not a closet. I don't use it. I use the one in the trailer."

"Well, how about me? Can I use the one in the trailer?"

"No, you stay out of there. If I ever catch you in there, you will be off to jail for sure."

"Okay then. How about I clean up the bathroom so I can use it?"

Jack couldn't think of anything better for her to do at the moment. He reasoned that it might keep her occupied and out of his hair so that he could get back to fixing his plane. "Sure, kid. Knock yourself out."

Jack went back to working on his plane while Ann turned her attention to the bathroom. She started by pulling out all the boxes. Most of them were practically empty, so Ann consolidated the contents into a few boxes and neatly stacked them in the corner. She found a roll of paper towels on a shelf above the toilet and used towels to wipe down the sink and mirror. She saved the toilet for very last. Ann gingerly lifted the lid to see what horrors awaited her. She was relieved to find that the bowl was fairly clean but was empty of water. She decided to ask Jack if it worked.

Ann left the bathroom and walked up behind Jack. He was bent over the wing again, in deep concentration this time, with a piece of sandpaper in his hand.

"Does that toilet work?"

Jack jumped up again, startled at the sound of her voice. "I told you not to sneak up on me like that again!"

Ann bit her tongue this time and decided to simply repeat the question. "I'm sorry, sir. I just wanted to know if the toilet worked. There's no water in it." She peered over his shoulder. "What are you doing anyway?"

Jack sighed in response to another question with an obvious answer. "What is this in my hand?"

"Sandpaper," said Ann.

"So what do you think I'm doing?"

"Well, I know you are sanding the patch. What I meant was, why are you sanding the patch?"

He was caught off guard and had an awkward feeling again. Jack considered the possibility that maybe she was just sincerely interested in what he was doing and not trying to intentionally annoy him. He wasn't used to engaging in conversation. For years he had kept mostly to himself, avoiding people in general when possible and kids at all costs.

"Oh, well, uh …" Jack stumbled to get out an explanation. "The first coat of dope dried, and now I'm sanding it smooth before applying another coat. I'll sand the next coat once it dries, before I can apply the primer. Then I'll sand that before I touch up the paint. When I'm done, you won't even notice that patch. And yeah, the toilet works. You just have to turn on the water valve."

"Oh," Ann said simply before turning and walking away without another word.

Jack watched her return to the bathroom. He shook his head, wondering whether he would really ever understand her, and then returned to his work.

***

Ann turned on the water valve near the floor at the back of the toilet and heard water filling the tank. She flushed several times to make sure the toilet was working to her satisfaction. Then she used the remaining paper towels to wipe up the floor the best she could. Ann looked around, inspecting her handiwork. Maybe it wasn't clean enough for her mother to approve, but at least it was usable now. Ann gathered the used paper towels and the empty boxes and carried them to the trash bin that was out in back of the hangar.

It was now past one o'clock, and Ann hadn't had anything to eat for lunch. Her stomach began to growl. She didn't want to bother Jack again, but she didn't know what else she could do. This time she called out instead of walking over to him.

"Sir!" She waited for a response, but he didn't acknowledge her. "Sir!" she said again in a louder voice.

"What is it now?"

"I've finished with the bathroom."

Jack got up from his work and walked over to the bathroom. Alarm gripped him. "Hey, what did you do with all my stuff?"

"Nothing. I just put everything together into fewer boxes and threw the extra boxes in the trash. I didn't throw anything of yours away."

"Oh," Jack replied in a surprised manner. "Well, okay then." Jack surveyed her work. He had to admit that the place was cleaner than it had been for years, and she had done a good job of organizing and stacking the boxes.

"I'm hungry. It's past one, and I haven't had any lunch."

"Well, I fed you breakfast, and I'm not feeding you lunch. You call it a day and go home and eat."

"Are you sure, sir?"

"Listen, kid. Aubrey said I had to let you work here. He didn't say for how long. He certainly didn't say that I have to feed you. Now get going and let me finish my work."

"Okay then. If you want me to do a better job cleaning, you'll need to get some cleaning supplies and a new broom."

"Get going," Jack replied in an annoyed voice.

Ann shrugged and made her way out the side door of the hangar. She hopped on her bike and was starting to ride off when Jack called after her. She stopped and turned to see him in the doorway.

"You did all right, " Jack said.

Ann cupped a hand by her ear pretending she hadn't heard him.

"Sorry, sir, I didn't hear you."

Jake raised his voice and grudgingly repeated himself. "I said, you did a good job!"

"Thank you, sir."

"Just don't be late tomorrow. Be here at five thirty sharp," Jack said gruffly, reverting back to his former self.

"Yes, sir!" Ann proceeded down the road on her bike with a smile breaking out on her face. She would be flying in no time.

Chapter 6

Beep! Beep! Beep!

The sound of the alarm woke Sarah from a sound sleep. With her eyes barely cracked open, she managed to make out the numbers on the clock sitting on her nightstand: 4:45 a.m. She hit the snooze button and pulled the covers over her head as she rolled back over in bed.

Ten minutes later, the beeping resumed, and the annoying sound seemed even louder than the first time. Sarah grabbed her pillow and smothered herself, trying to dim the incessant beeping. After a few seconds, she caved to the inevitable and shut off the alarm. It took her a minute to focus and remember why she was getting up at this ungodly hour. Then it came to her: she had to get Ann out of bed and get her off to Jack's before she got another phone call from the old grouch.

Sarah got out of bed, put on her robe, and shuffled off to Ann's room. She flipped on the light switch as she entered the room and called to Ann without even looking at her bed. "Ann. Ann, come on. Get up. You have to get to Jack's."

The silence in the room surprised Sarah—not a groan, not a complaint. It was only then that Sarah realized that Ann's bed was empty. For a moment she panicked, thinking Ann had run away, but then she heard noises in the kitchen below her. Sarah hurried down the stairs and into the kitchen to see Ann sitting at the table, calmly eating a bowl of cereal.

"Well, good morning," Sarah said, surprised.

Ann was just finishing her last spoonful. "Good morning, Mom," Ann said with her mouth still half full with cereal. "I have to get going." Ann rose from the table and took her bowl over to the kitchen sink. She took a last gulp of milk from the glass in her hand and placed the glass and bowl in the sink.

"Well, let me make you a lunch."

"I already did." Ann picked up a brown paper bag from the counter. "I made a cheese sandwich and packed an apple."

Sarah just stood in disbelief. She wasn't sure whether this was her daughter or whether aliens had landed during the night and replaced her with a replica. Sarah immediately grew suspicious. She knew there must be a motive behind Ann's sudden change of heart and attitude.

"All right, young lady. Just what is going on? Did you get into more trouble with Jack yesterday? Just what are you up to?"

"No. I didn't do anything," Ann said in a disgusted voice. "Why do you always assume that I did something wrong or that I'm up to something?"

"Because I know you well enough to know that when you start doing things without being told, you are up to something," Sarah replied.

"Mom, I have to go. I'll be late again," Ann pleaded.

"Okay then. Get going."

"Oh, one more thing before I go."

"Yes?" Sarah asked.

"I know I'm grounded, but would it be okay if I go to the library before I come home after Jack's?"

Sarah was even more confused now. Ann hadn't asked to go to the library for years. When she was younger, Sarah had taken her all the time, and Ann had read books voraciously, but since her father left, she had spent more time getting into trouble than reading.

"Please, Mom. I have to look some things up about airplanes for Jack." Ann reasoned that a little white lie at this point wouldn't hurt.

"All right. You can go to the library and then come straight home. Don't let me catch you out running around with those boys again." Sarah decided not to push the point of her daughter's sudden interest in reading.

"Thanks!" Ann yelled as she ran past her mother and out the front screen door, letting it bang against the jamb once again.

Sarah winced. "Stop banging that door!" she called after Ann.

***

Ann threw the lunch bag into the basket attached to the handlebars of her bike, hopped on the seat, and pedaled as fast as she could. She wanted to reach the hangar before Jack. Once again the eastern sky was turning beautiful shades of color as the sun began its transit above the horizon. Ann's pedaling slowed as she came around the final bend, and the hangar came into view. The lights of the hangar were already on, and the large sliding front hangar door was open. Jack's crop-dusting plane was sitting in front of the hangar. Ann took a quick glance at the watch on her arm: 5:26 a.m. She was a few minutes early but hadn't beaten him to the punch. Ann leaned her bike up against the hangar and entered through the side door.

"Good morning, sir," Ann said in a cheery voice. "What are you doing?"

Jack didn't bother to acknowledge the greeting and replied in a businesslike manner. "I'm getting ready to do a preflight inspection. You always check the airplane before you get in and fly."

Ann's curiosity rose. "What do you check? Can I watch?"

Jack had learned enough about Ann to know it would be useless to say no. She would just continue to pester him until he answered her questions. He simply nodded to her and motioned with his hand for her to follow him out to the plane.

Ann followed behind as Jack walked around the tail and the left wing and up to the side of the airplane.

"First we check the fuel. The fuel tank in this plane is in the top wing of the plane. See that glass sight tube up there, sticking out from the bottom of the top wing?"

Ann nodded.

"It's connected to the gas tank. You can see the fuel level in the tube."

Ann began to take a step backward toward the front of the plane in order to get a better view of the top wing and the sight tube.

"Stop," Jack said in a stern voice. "Look at where you're stepping."

Ann looked around her, but she didn't see why Jack was concerned.

"You are standing right in the arc of the propeller."

Ann looked at the two-blade propeller. One blade was pointed straight up in the twelve o'clock position, and the other blade was pointed straight down in the six o'clock position. Ann had stepped back to a position where she would have been hit squarely if the propeller had been rotating.

"Never stand or walk in the arc of the propeller, even if it isn't turning. Get used to walking around it, so you never accidently walk into a turning prop."

"That's happened?" Ann was shocked by the thought.

"You would be surprised how many times someone has come up to a plane with the engine running and walked right into the turning prop. Big airports are noisy, and someone might not even hear or notice that the engine is running. I've seen it, and it ain't a pretty picture. You can't be playing games around here. There are a lot of things that could hurt you if you aren't careful, so don't be touching things or getting into things you don't know anything about."

Ann made a mental note of Jack's warning as she stepped out of the propeller arc. "Yes sir," she said. She was glad Jack didn't know she had been carelessly sprawled out in the middle of the runway when Wild Bill had shown up. It was already clear to her that Jack didn't tolerate foolishness in general, let alone foolishness that might get someone hurt.

"Okay then. So you check the fuel level. Look up there. You can see the tube is full, which means the tank is full. Next you check the oil."

Jack stepped onto the ladder and reached up to a cap on the top of the plane. He screwed off the cap and showed Ann that a dipstick was attached to the bottom. He took a rag from his back pocket, wiped the dipstick clean, and then inserted it back into the opening. He withdrew the dipstick once again and stepped off the ladder to show her. "What does that say?" Jack asked her, pointing to a spot on the dipstick.

Ann could make out a word stamped onto the metal. "It says 'Full,'" she replied.

"Where is the oil level?"

Ann looked again. The oil clinging to the dipstick reached from the tip of the dipstick to just below the word. "Just below full."

Jack took the rag from his back pocket and wiped the dipstick clean. He showed it to her once again, pointing. "What does that say?"

Ann looked again and saw the word "Add" stamped lower on the dipstick, below the word "Full." "It says 'Add.'"

"That's right. So if the oil level gets to that point, you need to add oil to the engine. Oil is the lifeblood of the engine. Lose your oil, and the engine is going to seize up on you. You always check the oil before you fly."

"Got it!" Ann replied enthusiastically.

Jack picked up a small glass jar from the ground beside the base of the ladder. He showed Ann a fuel drain on the bottom of the engine and drained some gas into the jar. Jack raised the jar to eye level and carefully eyed the contents.

"What are you doing?" Ann asked.

"I'm checking the fuel for contamination. Sometimes water gets in the gasoline. The gas is lighter than the water, so if there is water in the fuel you will see it separate at the bottom of the jar. You also check to see if there's any dirt in the fuel."

Jack handed the jar to Ann. She examined it, mimicking Jack. It seemed clean to her, and she couldn't see any water separated out in the bottom of the jar.

"Now we do a walk around and check the tires, wires, and control surfaces." Jack started to walk around the airplane, first checking the left tire and then running his hand along the front edge of the lower left wing. He plucked at the wires that ran between the top wing and the lower wing as if they were strings on a harp, making sure they were under the correct amount of tension.

"What are control surfaces?"

"A plane has three axes of motion. You have the roll axis, the pitch axis, and the yaw axis. Come over here, and I'll show you."

Ann followed Jack around to the back of the left wing of the airplane. Jack lifted a part of the lower wing that was attached to the rest of the wing by a long hinge.

"This is an aileron. You have them on each wing, and they are connected. One goes up; the other goes down. Go around the plane and look at the right aileron."

Ann ran around the back of the plane and looked at the right wing. She could see that the right aileron was down. Jack moved the left aileron down, and the right aileron moved upward.

"If the left aileron is down, the force of the wind will lift the left wing up. At the same time, the right aileron is up, and the wind pushing on it will force the right wing down. That will cause the airplane to roll to the right. When they move in opposite directions, the plane rolls to the left."

Ann was becoming more and more engrossed as Jack continued with his explanation. She had never really considered how airplanes flew or how they were controlled. She also noticed that Jack took on a different demeanor when he was talking about flying. The gruffness seemed to leave him as he instructed her on the details of the flight control surfaces.

Jack moved to the tail of the plane and placed his hand on what looked like a little wing sticking out horizontally. "This is the horizontal stabilizer. An elevator is attached to the end of the horizontal stabilizer by a hinge so it moves up and down. Go ahead. Lift it up."

Ann gingerly placed her hands on the elevator. She was surprised that Jack was actually letting her touch the plane. She hesitated.

"Go ahead. Lift it."

Ann lifted the elevator upward.

"Now think. The wind is moving horizontally along the side of the airplane over the horizontal stabilizer and hits the elevator, which is sticking up. What's the elevator going to do?"

Ann surveyed the position of the elevator. "Well … if it works like the aileron … the wind will push the tail downward."

A small smile flashed ever so briefly across Jack's face. "That's right. The wind will push the tail downward, which will cause the nose of the plane to pitch upward. Push the elevator down, and the wind will pitch the tail upward, and the nose will pitch downward. That's how the pitch axis is controlled."

"What controls the yawn?" Ann inquired.

"That's *yaw*, not yawn," Jack replied, shaking his head. "The rudder controls yaw. See the portion of the tail sticking straight up in the air? That's the vertical stabilizer. The rudder is attached to the back of the vertical stabilizer with a hinge so it can move left and right."

Jack moved to the back of the plane and pushed the rudder to the right. "Now imagine the wind pushing on the rudder. Which direction will the tail go?"

"To the left!" Ann replied immediately.

"That's right. Now watch." Jack pushed the whole tail of the plane to the left. "What happens to the nose?"

"It went to the right."

"Exactly. Right rudder points the nose to the right. Left rudder points the nose to the left."

Jack continued his inspection along the right wing of the airplane, moving the right aileron up and down and checking the tension of the wires on the right wing. Ann tagged right along with him, careful to observe everything he was doing.

She noticed Jack had painted the repair patch with the silver primer but hadn't yet painted it yellow to match the rest of the plane. She ran her fingers over the patch. The patch blended so well with the rest of the wing that she could barely feel its edges. She was impressed with Jack's repair job.

Jack carefully examined the edges of the propeller as the pair came back around to the front of the plane. "You check the prop and make sure there are no nicks or cracks. A damaged prop is liable to go flying right off the airplane or break up into pieces."

"Geez, has that ever happened to you?"

"When you've been flying as long as I have, just about everything has happened to you. Stand back now."

Jack pushed the lower blade of the propeller counterclockwise until the other blade was in a position he could reach. He then grabbed that blade and pushed it counterclockwise until the first blade was back within his reach. He kept repeating this action until he had completely rotated the propeller several times.

"What are you doing?"

"I'm pulling the prop through to make sure the engine is free to rotate. This is a radial engine. See, the cylinders are arranged in a big circle." Jack pointed to one of several metallic objects that encircled the central core of the engine.

"The cylinders sort of look like those old glass milk jugs," Ann said, pointing upward.

"You aren't the only one who thinks so. A lot of people call the cylinders 'jugs.' Anyway, when the engine sits for a while without running, oil can accumulate in the lower cylinders. If you start it like that with too much oil in the cylinders, you will damage the engine. I'm pulling the prop through to make sure there isn't any accumulated oil in the cylinders, and the engine is free to rotate."

Ann looked over the plane, amazed that such a small plane would need so much attention just to get it started. "It seems to me like a lot of things can go wrong," Ann commented quietly.

Jack didn't bother to acknowledge her remark.

"What keeps it in the air? I mean, why doesn't it just fall out of the air if the engine stops or slows down?" Ann was thinking of the way Wild Bill's plane had continued to glide even when she heard the engine power reduced.

"The engine pulls the plane through the air. The force provided by the engine is called thrust. The wings, though, provide lift, and that's what keeps the airplane in the air—well, at least until gravity pulls it back down," Jack explained.

"Well, how do the wings provide lift?"

"Look at the side of the wing at the edge. You see how the upper surface is curved?"

Ann looked where Jack was pointing. She noticed that the bottom of the wing was essentially flat, but the upper surface of the wing had a curve.

"The shape of the wing causes the air flowing over the wing to move slower than the air moving under the wing. The difference in air flow causes the air pressure under the wing to be greater than the air pressure above the wing. The difference in pressure provides lift by essentially applying an upward force."

Ann nodded her head in agreement, although she wasn't sure she completely understood Jack's explanation.

"I'm going to start it up now and leave for my first dusting run. You get back in the hangar and stay there until I've taxied out to the runway. Make yourself useful while I'm gone. There are old tires under the workbench that I need to take to the dump. Put them in the back of my truck."

"Yes, sir."

"And don't touch anything else!" With that, Jack put on a flying helmet and flight suit similar to the ones Wild Bill had worn. He climbed into the cockpit as Ann walked back into the hangar. "Clear!" Jack called out.

The engine began to cough and sputter to life, blowing a cloud of white smoke back toward the hangar. Ann could see that Jack was doing something to cause the control surfaces to move back and forth, checking to make sure they worked properly. She wanted to know just how the pilot controlled them, but she felt lucky at the moment that Jack had even explained how they worked. She would ask him later to show her the inside of the cockpit. Ann watched as Jack taxied the plane to the end of the runway, turned, and gunned the engine. The fully loaded plane took a little longer to get off the ground than Wild Bill's, but Ann thought the takeoff was even more graceful. She watched as the plane flew off into the rising sun and the drone of the engine faded. She was hooked. She had to fly.

Chapter 7

A nn headed toward the hangar's side door to get her lunch bag out of the basket on her bike. As she passed through the door, she noticed a new broom leaning against the wall and a large brown bag on the floor. She smiled to herself. Jack had been listening to her. She proceeded to get her lunch bag from the bike and put it in the refrigerator. She noticed that the refrigerator hadn't been cleaned in a very long time and made a mental note to add it to the list of things she could do while Jack was out flying.

Ann took the brown bag by the broom to the workbench and unpacked it. There were paper towels and toilet paper on the top, followed by various cleaning products. To Ann's surprise, the bottom of the bag also contained a six-pack of Coca-Cola, which Ann also placed in the refrigerator beside her lunch bag.

Ann went to work picking up the old tires lying around the hangar and put them in the back of Jack's truck. They were much smaller and lighter than car tires, so Ann didn't have a problem lifting them up high enough to throw them over the tailgate. When she was finished with the chore Jack had given her, she used the cleaning supplies to clean the bathroom and refrigerator to a level that would have made even her mother proud.

Over an hour had passed when Ann was interrupted by the noise of something hitting the side of the hangar. She looked out the side door, which Jack usually left propped open to get a cross breeze in the hangar, to see the boys standing on the gravel road, throwing stones in her direction.

"Hey, jailbird!" Billy called out.

"What do you want now?"

"Why aren't you out flying?" Billy called back in a sarcastic voice. All the boys laughed together.

"Jack has a lot of work to do. He'll teach me later," Ann replied.

"Sure he will." The boys laughed again. "The only things that are flying around here are these stones."

Billy nodded to the other boys. They each reached down and picked up a gravel stone. On Billy's command, all three boys threw the stones in Ann's direction. Ann ducked back inside the hangar door. Two of the stones bounced off the outside wall of the hangar. The third flew through the open doorway and bounced harmlessly on the hangar floor. Ann picked up the stone, went out the door, took careful aim, and let fly with all her might.

Joey saw the stone coming and yelled out a warning to the other boys. Both he and Tommy ducked, but Billy just turned back in the direction of the hangar to see what was happening. The stone hit him squarely in the forehead.

"Ouch! I'm going to get you for that!" Billy shouted at Ann.

The loud rumble of an approaching plane announced Jack's return before Billy could take a step toward her. Tommy was the first to see it, and he pointed toward the sky in the direction of the approaching plane. "It's Jack. He's coming back. Let's get out of here!" Tommy yelled.

"This isn't over. I'll get you later!" Billy shouted at Ann angrily.

The boys hurried to get moving on their bikes as Jack's plane came flying over, no more than fifty feet above them. Ann watched as Jack banked the plane and lined it up with the center of the road, where the boys were now pedaling furiously to get away. To her amazement, the plane swooped low over the boys and released a plume of spray from the lower wing that encased the boys in a dense fog. When the fog lifted, she could see that they had run into one another and were sprawled all over the road. She couldn't help but let out a loud laugh at the boys' predicament.

Ann watched as Jack circled around the field and landed. She went back inside the hangar to watch him taxi up and waited for him to shut down the engine before running up to him. "That was great!"

"What?"

"It was great the way you dive-bombed them."

"I wasn't dive-bombing anyone. I just had a little wash water left in the tank that I needed to clean out before the next dusting run. What were those delinquents doing out here anyway? Were you letting them into my hangar while I was gone?" Jack eyed her suspiciously.

"No, sir."

"Then what were they doing here?" Jack repeated.

"They were here teasing me."

"About what?"

"They said girls can't fly. I told them that girls could fly just as well as any boy and that you were going to teach me."

"Well, you shouldn't have told them such a foolish thing. I told you I'm done with teaching," Jack said in an annoyed tone. "Did you pick up the tires?"

"Yes, sir. I cleaned the bathroom again and the refrigerator too."

Jack just grunted. "I need to fill up the hopper again."

"Can I help?"

Once again, Jack just motioned for her to follow him. Jack went over to the side of the hangar, where several fifty-five-gallon drums were stored. Jack placed a hand dolly under one of the drums and rolled it out to the side of the airplane. He showed Ann how to open the cap on the top and slide the base of a hand pump into the drum. Jack climbed up on the wing of the plane with a hose attached to the pump and placed the hose's nozzle into the opening of the hopper tank located in front of the cockpit.

"Start pumping, kid."

Ann grabbed the crank handle of the pump and began to move it in a circular motion with her right hand. It wasn't long before her right arm tired, and she had to shift to her left hand. Before much longer, she had to use two hands to keep the handle moving. Ann's arms felt like rubber by the time the drum was empty.

"Okay. Next one," Jack said.

"Another one?"

Jack jumped down from the wing, withdrew the pump from the empty drum, and fetched a new drum from the hangar. He attached the pump to the new drum and took his place again on the wing. "Start cranking."

Ann turned the crank once again as fast as she could. It wasn't long before she began running out of steam, and the rotation of the crank handle slowed to a crawl. Jack jumped down from the plane and motioned her away from the pump handle.

"That's the problem with all you kids nowadays," Jack huffed. "You're all soft from not doing any real work."

Ann watched as Jack rotated the pump handle with ease and kept the pace up until the entire drum was empty. She was surprised that the old man had that much energy in him. Jack finished with the second drum and once again did a preflight inspection of the airplane. He pulled on his flying helmet and climbed back into the cockpit.

"All right. You get back into the hangar so I can start up."

Ann stepped back within the threshold of the hangar door and watched as Jack started the plane and took off. It was only after he was gone that she realized he hadn't given her another chore. She also noticed that he hadn't given her his usual admonishment against touching anything. Having not been specifically prohibited from doing so, she felt this gave her some leeway to do a bit more exploring around the hangar. She would start with the little yellow plane with the high wing.

She had learned from her constant questioning of Jack while she worked that the little yellow plane was a Piper Cub and was often used as a trainer to teach people to fly. Ann walked over to the right side of the plane. A lower door panel was opened downward. A side window was opened upward and latched to a mechanism provided on the underside of the wing. With the window open and the door panel down, a large opening was provided in the side of the plane through which one could climb into the cockpit.

Ann noted that this plane was much different from the two-wing crop duster that Jack was flying. Jack had explained to her that planes with two sets of wings are called "biplanes," and planes with one set of wings are called "monoplanes." Besides having only one set of wings, this plane didn't have a big round engine in the front that you could see. Instead, the engine was entirely covered, like the engine of a car. Ann looked inside the cockpit. There were two seats, with one lined up behind the other. She looked nervously around the hangar to make sure she was alone and then climbed into the front seat.

The first thing Ann noticed was that she couldn't see out of the front of the airplane. The Cub, like the Stearman crop-dusting planes Jack and Wild Bill flew, was a tail dragger, and the nose of the airplane was pointing so high in the air that Ann couldn't see straight ahead. Several gauges were laid out on a small instrument panel in front of her. A control stick protruded between her legs. She placed her hands on the stick and moved it left and right. Ann saw that this caused the ailerons on the wings to move. She moved the stick back and then forward. She could hear something moving, but it wasn't readily apparent what she was controlling at first. She looked out the side of the plane back toward the tail. Moving the stick back and forward again, she noticed that the elevator's movement corresponded to the movement of the stick. She now understood how to control the ailerons and the elevator.

Ann continued to look around the cockpit and noticed two sets of pedals on the floor. She put her feet on the larger pedals and pushed back and forth. Looking back toward the tail through the side opening, she could barely see the movement of the rudder as she pushed the pedals. Next she placed her feet on the smaller pedals, which were closer to her. These were harder to push and didn't appear to cause any movement of the control surfaces. She decided she would find a way to ask Jack later about the purpose of the smaller pedals.

Ann was growing ever more interested in flying, not so much to impress the boys now or to prove a point but just out of sheer curiosity about what it must be like to fly among the clouds. When she saw an airliner pass overhead, she no longer wondered about the passengers and where they might be going, but instead she wondered what it would be like to actually be at the controls of a jet airliner flying so high and so fast. She had to find a way to get Jack to teach her to fly.

She knew, however, that having Jack find her sitting in the plane without permission would not be the best way to pursue her goal, so she carefully climbed out of the plane, making sure not to disturb anything. Ann decided she could score some points by showing she was responsible and taking some initiative. She had spied some old paint cans and brushes when she was pulling old tires out from under the workbench. Ann went through the cans now until she found one that seemed to be nearly full of white paint. Picking up one of the brushes, she went to work painting the faded walls of the bathroom with a fresh coat of bright white paint.

Ann had finished two of the four walls of the bathroom when she heard a car pull up outside. A minute later, someone called out, "Hello? Is anyone here?"

Ann recognized Aubrey's distinctive drawl. "I'm in here," Ann replied.

Aubrey peered in the bathroom door. By this time, Ann had managed to get almost as much paint on herself as on the walls. Her clothes, face, and sun-bleached brown hair were covered with splotches of white paint.

"So does Jack have you doing some painting, or are you changing your hair color?" Aubrey asked, laughing.

Ann wasn't amused by the comment. She wiped the sweat from her brow. "Actually, it was my idea to paint the bathroom. He isn't here, but I think he'll be back soon."

"Well, young lady, I have some official business with both you and Jack." This time Aubrey's voice was serious.

Ann certainly didn't like the words "official business" or the tone of Aubrey's voice. She braced herself for the bad news.

"Billy Henderson's mother called me and told me you nearly put his eye out with a rock today. Is that true?"

Ann's stomach tightened. "It wasn't a rock. It was just a measly ole little gravel stone. Besides, he threw it at me first! I was just returning it to him. I can't help it if he can't catch."

Aubrey gave her a look of disapproval. "Well, that may be your story, but he has a nice welt on his forehead, and his mother is really upset. I don't want to have to tell your mother about this and get you into trouble with her. How about you promise me you'll apologize to Billy in front of his mother on your way home tonight? I already told her I would talk to you and that you would apologize to Billy. I also told her it would never happen again."

The thought of apologizing to Billy made her sick to her stomach. The last thing she wanted, however, was for her mother to find out. She would be grounded for another month, and her mother would never let Jack teach her how to fly.

"Yes, sir," Ann replied meekly.

"You promise me you won't be throwing any more rocks ... er, stones, at anyone?"

"Yes, sir."

"Okay. I'm putting myself on the line for you, Ann, so don't let me down."

"Yes, sir. I won't."

Aubrey turned to go out the door but stopped short. The sound of Jack's plane coming in for a landing could be heard in the distance. He and Ann walked to the threshold of the large sliding door and waited for Jack to taxi the plane back to the hangar. Aubrey met Jack as he climbed down off the wing of the plane and took off his helmet.

"Good morning, Jack."

"Just what do I owe this visit to? Checking up on me, are you?" Jack grunted back.

"I see we are in a friendly mood as always, eh, Jack? Well, as a matter of fact, I'm out here on some official business with respect to both you and this young lady. I've already concluded my business with her, and now it's your turn."

"What do you want with me?"

"Billy Henderson's mother called and complained that you sprayed the boys with fertilizer this morning with your plane."

"Well ... you never know where those delinquents might be hanging around. If I'm spraying a field, and they aren't where they are supposed to be, they just might get sprayed."

Ann looked at Jack. He was staring straight ahead at Aubrey, not blinking an eye as he spoke.

"They were on the road, Jack, not near a field you were spraying."

"Like I said, if they are hanging around where they shouldn't be, then they are likely to get sprayed. Besides, it wasn't fertilizer. I was just rinsing out the tank and spray nozzles with some wash water. A little wash water never killed anyone."

"Okay, Jack. I'll take your word for it this time, and I'm going to let it go just this once. I've already told his mother that it was probably just an accident, but that I would speak to you about it. I know those kids are always out here bothering you, but that isn't the way to handle the situation. I like to consider myself a peace officer, Jack, more than a police officer. So let's all just work a little harder to keep the peace, and be a little more careful where you are spraying in the future. I'll tell those kids to stay away from your hangar in exchange."

Jack mumbled and cursed under his breath.

"Jaaaack?" Aubrey drew out his name as if addressing a little boy.

Jack stood still for several moments and then gave Aubrey a slight nod. Ann couldn't help but think that he looked like a little kid who'd gotten caught with his hand in the cookie jar.

"Okay then. I'm putting myself on the line for you too, Jack, so no more stone throwing and no more accidental spraying."

"What do you mean, stone throwing?" Jack had a puzzled look on his face.

Aubrey just pointed to Ann without saying a word.

"Oh?" Jack looked at Ann inquisitively.

"That has all been taken care of, right, Ann?" Aubrey gave Ann a stern look.

"Yes, sir. No more stone throwing," Ann replied.

Aubrey turned and walked out of the hangar without further comment.

***

Ann ran out of the hangar and caught Aubrey before he reached the car.

"Thanks, Aubrey, for not telling my mother."

"That's okay, Ann. Just try to stay out of trouble and say hello to your mother for me."

"Okay, and thanks for Jack too."

Aubrey smiled and drove off with a wave.

***

Ann returned to the hangar to find Jack standing in the bathroom, looking at the painted walls. He had a puzzled look on his face. "Who told you to paint?"

"No one. I just thought it would look a lot better, and you had some old paint lying around."

Jack took another look around and said nothing. He went over to the refrigerator, opened the door, and took out two of the Coca-Colas Ann had placed there earlier. He placed the lip of the cap of the first bottle on the edge of the workbench and hit the bottle with his free hand, causing the cap to pop off. He motioned for Ann to take the bottle. She took it from him, and he repeated the process with the second bottle. Jack raised the second bottle to his lips and took a long drink.

"That Henderson kid ratted us out," Jack said, wiping his mouth with his sleeve. "Seems like we are both fugitives from the law."

Ann smiled and took a long drink of her Coca-Cola.

Chapter 8

Ann and Jack fell into a daily routine. Ann would arrive in the morning and help Jack prepare the crop-dusting plane for the first flight of the day. Once he had taken off, she would turn to busying herself with whatever chore Jack had given her. Jack would return from his first run, and Ann would help him refuel the plane and fill the hopper for the next flight. Jack would take off again, and Ann would return to her chores.

Some days, Jack made four or five flights. Other days, the weather wasn't right for flying or crop dusting. Jack spent his time working on his plane on the off days while Ann watched and asked endless questions. When it came to flying, she had become a sponge, soaking up every bit of knowledge that Jack would bestow on her, but he remained firm in his refusal to teach her how to fly.

It was during one of the off days that Wild Bill dropped in for another visit. After spending so much time at Jack's, Ann could now recognize the low drumming beat of a big radial airplane engine coming from miles away. She was in the middle of helping Jack with an oil change when the beat began reverberating through the hangar. Ann dropped the empty oil cans she was carrying to the trash and ran out the front door of the hangar to see Wild Bill's plane coming into sight. He was approaching low and fast and heading straight for the runway. Her jaw dropped as Wild Bill roared down the runway no more than fifty feet in the air and did a complete roll of the airplane.

"Wow, did you see that?" she yelled out in excitement to Jack. She hadn't even realized that he had walked out and joined her to watch Wild Bill's plane fly by.

"I saw it. Crazy fool!" Jack huffed and went back inside.

Ann continued to watch as Wild Bill zoomed upward and turned, heading back in the opposite direction. She suddenly became aware of the oil all over her hands and face. For the first time in her life, she actually cared about her appearance. Ann ran into the hangar past Jack and into the bathroom, slamming the door behind her.

"Hey, pick up those oil cans and throw them away like I told you!" Jack yelled after her.

Failing to receive a reply, Jack bent down and started gathering up the empty cans, muttering to himself under his breath.

***

Ann looked in the mirror at her oil-covered face and disheveled hair. She quickly got the soap and tried washing her face and hands the best she could. Not having a brush or comb with her, the best she could do with her hair was run her fingers through it several times, trying to get out the knots. She was tucking her shirt into her jeans when she heard Wild Bill's plane taxi up to the hangar. He was here, and she was out of time. Ann took one last look in the bathroom mirror and ran back to the front of the hangar. Wild Bill had already gotten out of his plane and was shaking hands with Jack as Ann approached.

"Well, hello there, Miss Ann. You look very pretty today."

Ann could feel her cheeks warming as she blushed at the compliment. "Hello, Wild Bill."

"Is that a new kind of makeup you are wearing?" Wild Bill said, reaching out and rubbing a smudge of oil from her cheek that she had missed. "There you go. A pretty young lady like you doesn't need to wear any makeup."

Ann flushed with embarrassment.

"So how is your prison sentence going? Is Jack working you to the bone?"

"No. He's actually been teaching me a lot about airplanes. I want to learn how to fly. I want to be a pilot," Ann replied.

"You like flying, do you?"

"Well, I've actually never even been up in a plane, but it looks like a lot of fun. I would love to be able to fly above the clouds in one of those new jet airliners."

"Is Jack going to give you flying lessons?"

"I'm doing no such thing!" Jack appeared agitated by the question. "I've told her a million times I'm not teaching anyone to fly, and that includes her. She's here to work off her debt for damaging my plane, and the sooner she does, the sooner she can go."

"How much longer is that going to be, Jack?" Wild Bill asked, winking at Ann.

"Well, I ... er ..." Jack didn't have an answer to the question. Although he initially had objected to the idea of having Ann work around the hangar, he found he had become used to her presence and constant stream of questions. He would never admit it to anyone, but he had found it was actually nice to have someone around giving him a hand.

"It seems to me you are taking advantage of this young woman." Wild Bill looked around the hangar. "By the looks of this place, I'd say she has more than paid for a little patching and paint."

"Don't forget, I lost work too!" Jack snapped back. "Which, by the way, was to your benefit."

"That may be true, Jack, but don't you think she has evened the score? This place looks better than it has in years."

Wild Bill looked at Ann and gave her a wink. Ann's heart skipped a beat every time he looked at her with his deep blue eyes.

"Maybe you could give her a few lessons in exchange for her continuing to work around the hangar."

"That would be great!" Ann chimed in immediately. "I'll work extra hard, sir, and do anything you want me to do."

"What's going on here?" Jack said, staring at Wild Bill. "First, Aubrey blackmails me into letting her work off her debt, and now you are causing trouble by putting crazy ideas in her head. What do you think you are, anyway, her lawyer?"

"I'm just saying what's fair is fair, Jack. It wouldn't hurt for you to give the kid a lesson or two."

Jack turned his attention to Ann. "Listen, kid, if you want to go, that's fine with me. I didn't want you here in the first place. I can tell you one thing for sure: I'm not teaching you to fly, and that's final!" Jack turned and started toward his workbench.

"Okay, don't teach her, but let me give her a ride in the Cub," Wild Bill called after him.

Jack stopped in his tracks and turned toward Wild Bill. "I said don't start putting ideas in her head. I'm not letting you fly the Cub with her or anyone else. I taught you better than to be pulling stupid stunts like the one I just saw. One of these days, you are going to get into trouble, and I don't want her in the airplane with you when you do."

"Hey, I don't need to be lectured by you about my flying," Wild Bill replied.

"Well, evidently, you do. Who are you trying to impress by doing those stupid stunts, anyway? I taught you to fly responsibly, not like a jackass bent on killing himself."

"I taught aerobatics in the army air corps. I know what I'm doing!" Wild Bill said, clearly agitated.

"I don't care what you taught where. You don't take unnecessary risks flying low just to show off, and that's the only reason you're doing it—to show off! You'll end up like Douglas Bader or worse." Jack pointed his finger at Wild Bill for emphasis.

Ann was surprised at Jack's expression of concern over both Wild Bill's safety and her own. Ann realized, even if Wild Bill didn't, that Jack wasn't just a grouchy old man complaining. He was seriously worried about Wild Bill's safety and hers. He cared.

Wild Bill just waved at Jack as if his hands could deflect Jack's oncoming words. "You are changing the subject. We aren't talking about me; we are talking about Ann. She's been working her behind off for you. The least you can do is let me give her a ride if you won't."

It was Jack's turn to wave dismissively. He ignored Wild Bill and continued to the workbench, where he busied himself with some task while grumbling under his breath.

"Well, I'm sorry, Miss Ann. I tried. I would give you a ride in my plane, but there's no room for you."

"It's okay." Ann was discouraged, but she wasn't about to give up. She was determined to find some way to change Jack's mind.

"Fifty cents an hour," Jack called out from the workbench without turning around.

"What was that, Jack?" Wild Bill replied.

"I'll give her fifty cents an hour and not one penny more. Take it or leave it."

Ann looked at Wild Bill in amazement. "I'll take it!" Ann said with a smile. "Thanks, Wild Bill."

"Well, I say we should celebrate your change in status from prisoner to employee. How about we have a little fly-in here on Saturday?"

"What do you mean?"

"I'll ask a few friends to fly over in their planes, and we'll have a picnic and do some flying. I'm sure we can wangle a plane ride for you out of one of them."

"Really? That would be great!"

"You can ask your mom to come, and I can see if she is as pretty as I remember."

"Oh." Ann couldn't help but feel a little deflated, and she wondered if Wild Bill was just humoring her to get in good with her mother.

"I'm sure your mom must be beautiful to have a daughter as pretty as you."

Wild Bill winked at her again, but this time it had no impact. Ann just nodded.

"Okay. You go sweet-talk Jack into it, and I'll make a few phone calls when I get back home."

Wild Bill hopped back into his plane and took off, leaving Ann standing in front of the hangar door. She watched until his plane was just a tiny speck in the sky and then went over to talk with Jack.

"Can we have a fly-in on Saturday like Wild Bill suggested?" Ann asked Jack. "I could ask my mom to come. She makes great potato salad."

Jack just continued working without acknowledging Ann.

Ann continued, "We could cook some hot dogs. You could even use your torch."

Jack put his tools down and turned toward Ann. "Just why would I want a bunch of people over here bothering me?" Jack asked.

"To have some fun? Pleeeeassse."

"I don't care what you and Bill do. I ain't paying you to fool around here on a Saturday—I'll tell you that right now."

"No, sir. I wouldn't expect to be paid. It's a *picnic*—you know, to have *fun*."

"Have it your own way. Just leave me out of it," Jack grumbled and turned back to his work.

"Sir?"

"What now?" Jack said in an annoyed tone.

"You said that Wild Bill would end up like someone named Bader. Who is Bader?"

"Douglas Bader. He was a British fighter pilot in World War II. He considered himself a real hotshot pilot before the war and was full of himself, thinking he could do anything with an airplane. Well, one day he was fooling around, doing aerobatics at low altitude, and crashed. He lost both of his legs in the accident."

"That's terrible. But how could he fly a plane in the war if he lost both of his legs?" Ann asked Jack.

"Bader was never one to give up. He had artificial legs fitted and learned to fly with them. The Royal Air Force tried to force him to take a desk job, but he fought to get back on flying duty. He won and got to fly a Hawker Hurricane fighter. He went on to shoot down twenty enemy planes, all the time flying without real legs."

"Wow. Really?"

"Yes, really. Are you calling me a liar?" Jack looked annoyed.

"No, sir. What happened to him?"

"He was finally shot down and taken prisoner by the Germans. Ironically, they think his plane was mistakenly hit by fire from one of his own men. They call that 'friendly fire,' when your own side shoots you down." Jack stopped to reflect for a moment. "I always thought that was a strange name for it, considering it ain't all that friendly to shoot down your own people. Anyway, he ended up trying to escape four times but never made it. He sat out the rest of the war as a prisoner."

"That's really some story."

"Sometimes real life is better than fiction. Now get going. Isn't it time for you to go home and stop bothering me?"

Ann made a mental note of the name Bader. She would go to the library and look him up as soon as she had a chance.

"Thanks, sir, for the fly-in. It will be fun. You'll see." Ann started out the door.

"Does it have mustard?" Jack called out.

"What?" Ann said, surprised by the question.

"Does your mother put mustard in the potato salad?"

"Yes, sir."

"I like mustard," Jack said matter-of-factly.

Ann just smiled and left Jack to his work.

Chapter 9

"Come on, Mama!" Ann called up the stairs. She was anxious to get out to the airfield before anyone else arrived.

"I'm coming. I'm coming. There's no need to yell."

Ann watched as her mother appeared and made her way down the stairs. She was wearing a bright yellow sundress and had her shoulder-length hair tied back with a ribbon. Ann couldn't help but think how young and pretty she looked. She had always thought her mother was beautiful, and she was just plain by comparison.

"You look nice, Mom."

"Well, thank you, Ann. Did you put everything in the car?"

Ann nodded and pulled her mother by the hand. "Come on. We don't want to be late."

When Sarah pulled their old Studebaker up beside the hangar, Ann was relieved to see that no one had arrived yet. She helped her mother get the things out of the car that they had brought for the picnic, including the potato salad and some folding chairs. They walked in through the side door and were met by Jack.

"Hello, Jack. Thank you for inviting me," Sarah said with a smile.

"I didn't invite you. It was your kid's idea. Well, it was hers and Bill's anyway," Jack replied in his usual gruff voice.

"Well, in any case, I'm glad to be here. Where should I put this?" Sarah asked.

Jack motioned to a makeshift picnic table sitting outside the front of the hangar. Ann had pestered Jack all week long about participating in the fly-in. She had finally gotten him to agree to put up a makeshift table and benches using some sawhorses and boards she had found stacked along the back wall of the hangar. He had even agreed to cook some hot dogs using an improvised grill made from his cooking sheet and his trusty torch. All they needed now were the guests.

It wasn't long before Wild Bill showed up. Ann was slightly disappointed when he landed without fanfare and parked his plane along one side of the grass runway. She had expected him to perform one of his usual flying tricks. Ann watched as he unloaded a few bags from the baggage compartment and walked toward the hangar.

"Who's that?" Sarah asked.

"That's Wild Bill," Ann replied. "He's a crop duster like Jack."

Jack approached them and set the bags down on the table. "Well, hello there, Miss Ann. You are looking pretty as usual today." Wild Bill turned his attention to Sarah. "This must be your lovely sister."

Ann was slightly annoyed by his obvious pandering and replied in a matter-of-fact tone. "This is my mom."

"Ah, Mrs. Wilson. Or should I say Miss Sarah Franklin? Don't you remember me?" Wild Bill reached out and took Sarah's right hand into both of his.

"Of course, I remember you, Bill. It's been a long time. How have you been, and how is your brother's eye?"

Ann was shocked by her mother's own confirmation that she had socked a boy in the eye.

Wild Bill threw his head back and laughed out loud. "My brother is just fine. He's married now with three kids."

"That's nice to hear, Bill," Sarah replied.

"My friends call me Wild Bill now, a nickname I picked up in the army air corps."

"Wild Bill?" Sarah laughed out loud, pulling her hand away. "Kind of a silly name for a grown man with the last name of Hickok, don't you think?"

"Well, my parents didn't do me any favors by naming me William in the first place, and I guess the guys in the squadron thought it was pretty funny. It just sorta stuck."

Ann had assumed Bill's nickname stemmed from the way he flew. Like her mother, she thought it was funny that it really referred to an old Wild West character.

Wild Bill turned to Ann for a moment. "Ann, I brought some Cokes in the bags there. Why don't you put them in the refrigerator while I talk to your mother?"

Ann could see she was being dismissed so that Wild Bill could turn his attentions and charm on her mother. She gave him a disgruntled look, but Wild Bill didn't notice. He had already turned his back to Ann and was talking with Sarah. Ann picked up the bags and headed for the refrigerator. It suddenly occurred to her that Wild Bill was a lot like her father. They were both handsome, dashing, and flirtatious, but they were also both irresponsible. She looked back to see her mother smiling and laughing at Wild Bill's jokes. She suddenly felt uncomfortable with the attention he was lavishing on her.

***

Ann was loading the Coca-Colas into the refrigerator when Aubrey came through the door carrying a brown bag. She had seen him in town during the week and invited him to the fly-in. Ann noticed he wasn't wearing his uniform but instead was dressed in pressed slacks and a crisp white shirt. His attire looked a bit dressy for a picnic to Ann.

"Hi, Ann. How are you doing? I brought some chips and pretzels." Aubrey held out the bag to her. "Is your mother here with you?"

She took the bag from Aubrey and noted the nervous tone in his voice and the way he was adjusting his belt. "Yeah, she's over there, talking to Wild Bill." Ann pointed toward the picnic table.

Aubrey looked out and saw Sarah and Wild Bill talking. "Oh." Aubrey stood in the doorway, shuffling his feet with an air of defeat about him.

Ann noticed the look of disappointment on his face. She then had her second revelation of the day. Ann walked over to him.

"Aubrey, can I ask you something?"

"Sure, Ann."

"Do you like my mom?"

"Well, of course, I like your mom. We were friends in high school."

"No. I mean, are you sweet on my mom?"

Aubrey blushed at the question and didn't answer. She didn't need to hear his reply to know that the answer was yes.

"Why don't you go over and talk to her?" Ann said, nudging him.

"Well … I … she's busy talking with Bill. I don't want to bother her."

A few other planes had already landed on the field by the time Aubrey arrived.

"Wait a second," Ann said to Aubrey.

She went out and put the bag Aubrey had given her on the picnic table and grabbed Wild Bill's hand. She started pulling him away from her mother and toward one of the airplanes that had just parked. "Come on, Wild Bill. I want you to show me the other airplanes. You promised to get me a ride!"

"I will in a minute, Ann. Your mother and I are talking."

Ann tugged a little harder. "You promised."

"Go ahead, Bill. I know Ann is really excited about seeing the airplanes, and you did promise her a ride. She's been talking about it all week long," Sarah said, smiling sweetly.

"Okay. I'll be back in a minute, though."

"I'll be here," Sarah replied.

Ann and Wild Bill walked out toward the grass runway in the direction of a little red biplane that had just landed and parked.

***

Aubrey remained in the hangar, nervously shuffling back and forth.

"Well?"

Aubrey hadn't even noticed Jack over by the workbench, fiddling with his makeshift grill, but he had been quietly listening to the conversation and observing.

"Well what?" Aubrey replied.

"Well, go talk to her. Can't you tell the kid is getting rid of the competition for you?"

Aubrey hesitated.

"I guess the old saying is true—youth is wasted on the young." Jack snorted and returned his attention to cooking some hot dogs on the grill.

Aubrey walked up to Sarah and quietly stood beside her without saying a word. After a moment, Sarah noticed him by her side.

"Well, hello, Aubrey. You look very nice today."

"Thank you, Sarah. That's a pretty dress you are wearing," Aubrey replied nervously.

***

Ann and Wild Bill were almost to the plane when she snuck a look back and saw Aubrey talking to her mother. A coy smile crossed her face.

"Hey, Bill. Who is that with you?"

Ann turned her attention back to the small red biplane. Unlike Jack's crop-dusting plane, this one had two cockpits. Ann was surprised to see a woman getting out of the front cockpit with a parachute strapped to her back. She was pretty and petite with dark flowing hair.

"Ann, this is Joe and Caroline Rinker. Joe and Caroline, meet Ann, Jack's new employee."

"Well, hello there, Ann." Joe shook Ann's hand.

"Hi, Ann. Wild Bill has told us all about you," Caroline said as she took off her parachute.

Ann couldn't help but wonder what exactly Wild Bill had told Joe and Caroline. She hoped he hadn't said anything about her damaging Jack's plane.

"Ann, Joe was a fighter pilot in World War II. He volunteered to fly for the British before the United States even got into the war. His Spitfire was shot down over France by none other than Adolf Galland, one of Germany's top fighter aces, during the Battle of Dunkirk."

"Pleased to meet you, Mr. Rinker."

"You can call me Joe, like everyone else."

"Caroline was in the French underground resistance. She found Joe when he was shot down and hid him from the Germans for weeks in a barn. Later she helped him escape back to England, where he went on to fly P-51 Mustangs with the army air corps."

"Wow. You were like a secret agent?"

"Well, not quite, but we all tried to do our part," Caroline replied with a lilting French accent.

"Caroline is being modest. The Germans would have killed her and her family if they had caught her. Pretty brave stuff just to save this worthless guy's behind." Wild Bill gave Joe a playful punch in the arm, hard enough to knock him slightly off-balance. "Joe went back after the war and found her, married her, and brought her back here to the States."

Ann thought about what Jack had said—real-life stories were sometimes much better than anything someone could make up. "That sounds romantic," Ann said to Caroline.

"Well, it is not so romantic when he comes in from the hangar covered with grease and leaves his clothes all over the floor or when he won't take out the trash."

"Oh, honey." Joe gave Caroline a playful hug.

"Okay, let me go. I see there is actually another woman here besides Ann and myself."

"That's my mom."

"I'm going to go say hello. We girls need to stick together among all these crazy guys. You remember that, Ann." Caroline smiled at Ann. "Joe, why don't you take her for a ride?"

"Really?" Ann exclaimed. She couldn't contain her excitement.

"Wild Bill said you were chomping at the bit to get a plane ride," Joe replied. "How about I take you up for some aerobatics?"

"I'll have to ask my mom first."

"I already did," Wild Bill said. "She said it was okay for you to go."

"Thanks, Wild Bill."

"No problem, kid." Wild Bill looked back toward the hangar and saw Aubrey and Sarah talking. "Looks like I should be getting back anyway. You enjoy the ride."

Ann watched as Wild Bill jogged back toward the hangar and her mother.

"Okay, Ann. Let me show you how to put on Caroline's parachute." Joe helped Ann into the parachute and carefully explained to her how it operated.

The thought of having to jump out of an airplane terrified Ann, and it must have showed on her face.

"We really won't be needing this unless a wing folds up. Don't worry, that is highly unlikely. But it is always better to be safe than sorry," Joe said in a reassuring tone.

Ann nodded her head, but she didn't like hearing about the possibility of a wing folding up. "What kind of plane is this?" Ann asked.

"It's a Pitts Special. It was built specifically for aerobatics. It's plenty strong, and we won't be doing anything she wasn't specifically made to do. We'll go up to about three thousand feet and do a few loops, rolls, and stalls. Are you game?"

"You bet!" Ann said excitedly.

Joe helped her climb into the front cockpit and buckle the seat belt and shoulder harness. He had her put on Caroline's cloth helmet and goggles. "Now the helmet is equipped with a headset that has earphones and a microphone, so I'll be able to talk with you, and you can talk with me. Keep the microphone as close as possible to your mouth. If you get a little queasy, don't be afraid to say so."

Joe showed Ann how to plug the headset into audio jacks provided on the panel in front of her. He then climbed into the rear cockpit and started the engine. A moment later, Ann heard his voice in the earphones. "Are you with me? Can you hear me?"

"Yes, I can hear you."

"Okay then, here we go!"

Joe gunned the engine and rolled the plane forward. He lined up with the center of the runway and applied full power. The little airplane raced down the runway much faster than Jack's and Wild Bill's crop-dusting planes. They were off the ground in an instant and climbing at a high rate of speed toward the clouds high above. Ann was exhilarated and anxious at the same time. Joe leveled out the airplane at what he explained was three thousand feet.

"Ready to do a loop? Give me a thumbs-up."

Ann nodded her head and gave the thumbs-up signal. Joe immediately placed the plane into a dive to gain speed. Ann saw the ground rushing up toward them. She could hear the wind whistling through the wires stretched between the wings as they went faster and faster. Joe suddenly leveled the plane and started the loop by pulling up. Ann could feel herself being pressed into the seat as the view of the ground disappeared, and all she could see was the sky ahead of her. As they approached the top of the loop, Joe told her to look out to the left. She looked out to the end of the wing and saw the sky and ground switching positions as they reached the peak of the loop. Ann momentarily felt weightless and realized she was hanging upside down, held in place only by the seat belt and shoulder harness. As the plane arched over the top and continued downward, Ann could feel the pull of gravity pushing her back into the seat again as Joe completed the loop. It was only then that Ann realized she had been screaming with pleasure the whole time.

"Wow! That was better than any roller coaster ride!"

Joe laughed. "How about a spin?"

Ann nodded again.

"Okay. I'm going to slow the airplane down until we stall. A stall in an airplane means that air isn't flowing over the wing anymore, and there's no lift. Don't worry, the engine doesn't quit running like when a car stalls. It's an aerodynamic stall. The wing will drop, and the plane will enter a spin. We'll go around a few times and pull out. Are you game?"

It sounded scary to Ann, but she felt she could trust Joe. She gave the thumbs-up signal and pulled the seat belt tighter across her lap.

Joe started to slow the airplane down. Ann noticed that the nose was getting higher and higher. Suddenly, she felt a slight lurch, like the bottom had dropped out from under her, and the left wing dropped. Before she could say a word, the plane was turning to the left, and the nose was pointed downward. The plane went around once, twice, three times. Suddenly, the spin stopped, and Ann was looking directly at the ground. Joe pulled the plane up, and Ann could feel herself being pressed back in the seat again until they were level.

"What did you think?"

"That was a little scary, but it wasn't as bad as I thought."

Joe laughed again. "Are you ready for a roll?"

Ann immediately gave the thumbs-up signal again. Joe rolled the plane to the left and did a complete revolution. He then rolled the airplane to the right and did another complete revolution. Ann wasn't quite ready for the second roll, and she got a bit disoriented and dizzy.

"You okay?"

"I'm … I'm okay," Ann called out.

"It's all right to call it. A lot of people get dizzy the first time. No shame in calling it a day."

"Thanks, Joe. I'm ready to go back."

Joe headed back to the field and did a smooth, straight-in approach to the runway. He taxied back over to his parking place and shut down the engine. Ann had to sit a moment in the cockpit and get oriented. When she was ready, Joe helped her climb out and take off the parachute and helmet.

"What did you think?" Joe asked.

"I loved it! It was great. I have to learn how to fly!" Ann shouted. She saw her mother standing near the plane with Jack and ran over to them. "Did you see, Mom?"

"Yes, I did. Weren't you afraid?" Sarah said in a concerned voice.

"Well, just a little at first, but it was great!"

"I told you she would be fine," Jack said matter-of-factly. "Joe's an excellent and safe pilot. He doesn't take any unnecessary chances."

"Well, that's a real compliment coming from you, Jack." Joe nodded to Jack.

"Now if you two are done fooling around, there are some hot dogs up there on the table," Sarah said.

Ann took her mother's hand and walked up toward the hangar. She couldn't imagine a better day—unless, of course, she were doing the flying.

Chapter 10

A nn was euphoric from her first airplane ride and no longer cared what the boys thought of her or her boast to them about learning to fly. Between the time she spent at the hangar with Jack and being grounded at home, she hadn't seen or talked with the boys in days. They in turn stayed away from the hangar, no doubt for fear of either being pelted by stones or being dive-bombed from the sky. She wanted to learn how to fly more than ever now, since getting her first ride with Joe.

She had cleaned and organized the hangar to the point that it was almost as neat and orderly as in the picture she had found in the cabinet. Jack had even let her wipe down his tools and arrange them neatly in his tool chest and on hangers on the wall behind the workbench. The only things she had yet to touch were the dusty tarps covering the plane in the far corner of the hangar. She had asked Jack if he wanted her to take the tarps out and wash off the dust and grime, but Jack had told her to stay away from the plane and leave things the way they were. Jack had made it clear that touching that particular airplane was strictly forbidden, although he never would say why. Ann, however, was dying of curiosity to get a look at the mystery plane hidden beneath the tarps. She hadn't been near it since the day she first snuck into the hangar. Now with Jack out flying and nothing left for her to do, she couldn't help but sneak a look.

Ann picked up one of the flashlights from where Jack kept them on the workbench and went over to the covered plane. She could tell from the way the tarps hung from the wings like curtains that the plane was probably a biplane like the one Jack used for crop dusting. She carefully considered how she should approach her target to get a better look without disturbing the tarps. Ann decided she would take a look at the front of the plane first and see if it had a radial engine like Jack's crop duster.

Ann carefully lifted the tarp covering the front portion of the airplane and slipped underneath. She clicked on the flashlight. The bulb was dim at first, until she shook the flashlight and hit the base with her hand a few times to get the batteries to make better contact. As the bulb grew brighter, she could make out the front of the engine through a circular opening around the propeller. It was a radial engine like the one in Jack's crop-dusting plane, but instead of being open to the elements, this engine was enclosed by a metal cover like the Cub and Joe's Pitts. She had learned from Jack that the cover was called a cowling, and it help to improve the flow of air around the airplane, making it more streamlined. Ann carefully withdrew herself from under the tarp, making sure that it looked undisturbed.

Next, Ann approached the side of the plane and pulled back the tarp covering the cockpit area. She wasn't tall enough to see over the side. She was hesitant, however, to climb up on the wing of the plane for fear of causing damage, so she went back and got the stool that Jack kept in front of the workbench. She carefully climbed on top of the stool and took a peek over the side. The plane had a control stick and rudder pedals just like the Cub. The instrument panel contained some of the same instruments that she had seen in the Cub along with a few additional gauges.

To Ann's surprise, this plane wasn't a crop-dusting plane but instead had a second cockpit where the hopper was located in Jack's crop duster. Holding on to the edge of the rear cockpit with one hand and gripping the flashlight with the other, she leaned forward, trying to get a better look at the front cockpit. She was just about in a position to see when she felt the stool sliding out from under her. She dropped the flashlight, which bounced off the wing and onto the floor, and instinctively reached out with her hand to grab something to hold onto. The nearest thing to her was the edge of the tarp covering the wing. Ann grasped the tarp as she fell, pulling it down with her.

Ann sat dazed on the floor and surveyed the scene around her. She quickly looked at the wing where the flashlight had hit. Miraculously, she couldn't see any damage. The stretched fabric had bounced the flashlight off just like a trampoline. There wasn't even a nick in the paint. Ann had learned from Jack that fabric wings were actually incredibly strong in one aspect called shear strength, which meant they could support a load that was many times their weight. A person could actually stand on them or walk on them, as old-time barnstormers often did, but they also could be easily punctured by any sharp object, as Ann had learned from her screwdriver incident.

She sighed in relief until she realized that the tarp had slid completely off the wing and was now in a heap on the floor. Ann sat trying to think of a way to put the tarp back on the airplane, but it seemed there was no easy way she could get it back on by herself, given its weight and size. She was stumped.

Suddenly, the drone of Jack's engine vibrated through the hangar. He was back from his latest run. Ann began to panic. The flashlight had rolled under the plane when she fell. She crawled under the plane and picked up the flashlight to return it to the workbench, grabbing and dragging the stool along the way. Running back to the plane, Ann threw the tarp over the cockpit and tried to arrange it as fast as she could, quickly moving back and forth from one side of the plane to the other, tugging and pulling.

Jack's plane was now taxiing up to the hangar. Ann gathered up as much of the tarp that had fallen from the wing as she could hold in her arms and attempted to throw it back over the top of the plane. The upper wing of the plane, however, was more than ten feet in the air. The tarp hit the edge of the top wing and fell back down on Ann. She desperately tried again, but the result was the same. She just didn't have the physical strength and size to fling the heavy tarp over the wing.

Ann suddenly became aware of the dead quiet around her. She turned around to see Jack staring at her from the threshold of the main hangar door, with his flying helmet dangling from his hand. He had a stunned looked of disbelief on his face.

"What are you doing?" Jack shouted at her. "I told you to stay away from that plane!"

"I'm sorry. I just wanted to take a peek, and I accidently pulled the cover off."

"Accidentally? Accidentally? Like the way you accidently snuck into my hangar? Like the way you accidently damaged my plane?" Jack yelled in a furious voice.

"I'm sorry. I'll help you put the tarp back on."

"Don't touch anything. You haven't learned a thing, just like the rest of those delinquents that you run around with. I want you out of here. Now!"

"But … what about me helping you?"

"You've helped enough. Get out of here! I don't need you around. I don't need anyone around here bothering me. I should have known better than to trust you. Don't ever come back."

Ann dropped the tarp and ran from the hangar. Jumping on her bike, she pedaled as fast as she could all the way home. She dropped the bike in the front yard and ran upstairs, letting the screen door bang behind her.

***

Sarah heard the bang and looked at the clock in the kitchen. It was only 8:50 a.m. She went to the steps and called up. "Ann? Ann? What are you doing back so soon?"

Ann didn't answer, but Sarah could hear her daughter crying behind the closed bedroom door. She climbed the stairs and knocked softly on the door.

"Ann? Are you all right?" she asked in a gentle tone.

"Go away! Go away!" Ann pleaded.

Sarah ignored the plea and opened the bedroom door. Ann lay across the bed, sobbing uncontrollably.

"Ann! What's the matter?" Sarah sat down beside Ann on the bed and gently rubbed her back. "What's the matter, Ann? … Tell me."

"Oh, Mama. I ruin everything."

"Whatever do you mean, Ann?"

"I worked hard. I really tried," Ann sobbed.

"What happened, Ann? Did Jack hurt you?" Sarah grew concerned.

"No, no. I just wanted him to like me so he would teach me to fly. I tried being good. I tried to do everything I was supposed to do, but I ruined it. I ruin everything."

"What did you do, Ann?"

"I shouldn't have touched the plane, Mama. I just wanted to see what it looked like. He told me to leave it alone, but I didn't."

Sarah was confused. "What plane? I thought you were helping him with his plane."

"Not the Stearman or the Cub. The one covered up in the far corner of the hangar," Ann explained between sobs.

"Oh … I see. Now Jack's mad at you?"

"He said to never come back. He's really mad at me."

Sarah stroked her daughter's soft hair. "It's okay. I thought you didn't want to go there in the first place. And why was Jack so upset about you touching his plane? Did you damage it? It certainly doesn't sound like a hanging offense."

"No, I didn't damage it. But he told me to stay away from it. I think it was his son's. He was killed in the war. Jack keeps the plane covered up in the corner of the hangar. I just wanted to take a look and see what it was like."

"Well, it sounds to me like that plane must mean a lot to Jack. Maybe the plane is something he keeps to remember his son in a good way, or maybe he keeps it covered because looking at it reminds him of his son's death in a bad way. Whatever the case, if he told you to stay away from it, then you should have respected his wishes."

"I know, Mama. I shouldn't have gone near it." Ann managed to get the words out between gasps for breath.

"And what's all this about you learning to fly?"

Ann's sobbing had subsided to sniffles as she sat up in her bed. "I really want to learn how to fly, Mama, but I ruined it now. Jack won't ever change his mind. He'll never teach me. I ruined it just like I ruin everything."

"Ann, what do you mean, you ruin everything?"

"I'm sorry, Mama. I ruined your life. If I hadn't been born, you wouldn't have had to leave town. You could have finished school. You have to work so hard, and it's all my fault."

"Ann! Don't you ever say that or think that again. You didn't ruin anything. Life doesn't work out the way you plan or hope for sometimes, but that's just the way of the world. It's true that I had a lot of dreams as a little girl that didn't come true, but the most important dream did— having you." Sarah hugged Ann. "I wouldn't change a thing."

Ann hugged her mother back harder than Sarah could ever remember. She could feel tears welling up in her own eyes.

"Now, why don't you take a little time to settle down and dry those tears. I have a few errands to run. Why don't you come with me, and we can have lunch at the drugstore and an ice cream for dessert. After all, we should look on the bright side—it seems you have been released from your jail sentence!"

Ann smiled and let out a small giggle. "Well, he's not the most pleasant person to have to spend your time with every day."

"Actually, from what I know about Jack, I would say that is a compliment. I would much prefer to spend my time with Wild Bill!" Sarah laughed and winked at Ann.

"Mama!"

Sarah just laughed again and left Ann's bedroom, closing the door behind her. She went into her own bedroom to get her purse from on top of her dresser. She was about to leave the room when she paused and went to her closet instead. Opening the closet door, Sarah reached up for a small shoe box that she kept on the top self. She sat down on the bed and opened the lid of the box. It was filled to the top with various souvenirs from her youth.

Sorting through the contest ribbons and Girl Scout badges, Sarah found what she was looking for at the very bottom of the box and withdrew the item, which was wrapped in a small, dirty piece of cloth. Sarah carefully opened the folds of the cloth to reveal an old aircraft spark plug. A smile came across her face. She sat remembering the day she had snuck into Jack's hangar many years ago on a dare from none other than Aubrey himself. It seemed the old saying was true: the apple doesn't fall far from the tree.

Chapter 11

Ann woke up the next morning later than she had in weeks. There was no need for her to get up early anymore since Jack had banished her from the hangar. She didn't feel rested, however, because she had tossed and turned all night long. She lay in bed thinking about what had happened the day before and wishing she hadn't let curiosity get the better of her. If she had just listened to Jack, maybe she still would have had a chance to learn how to fly. Ann knew that she had been wrong and felt she needed to make things right somehow.

She got up and opened the top drawer of her dresser. She rummaged through the neatly folded pairs of socks and pulled out one sock from the back of the drawer that was tied shut at the top. Ann shook the sock and listened to the jingle of coins. The sock was her version of a safe deposit box. Ann dumped the contents of the sock out on the bed and carefully counted the coins: $2.79. It was all she had at the moment. She hadn't even received her first pay from Jack when he banned her from the hangar. She hoped it would be enough.

Ann put the change back in the sock and shoved it into the rear pocket of her jeans. She ran down the stairs and out the front door. Instead of running straight down the porch steps to her bike, however, she stopped and caught the screen door before it banged on the jamb. After gently closing the screen door, Ann ran down the porch steps, jumped on her bike, and started off for the center of town.

Ann jumped her bike over the curb and came to a screeching halt in front of the hardware store. She leaned the bike up against the front window of the store and ran inside, where she was greeted by the owner of the store, Mr. Edwards. Ann had been in the store several times with her mother, buying various items to fix up the house, and Mr. Edwards knew her by name.

"Hello there, Ann. How are you this lovely morning?"

"Good morning, Mr. Edwards. I need a screwdriver."

"Well, I'm sure I can help you with that. What kind of screwdriver do you need?"

Ann thought for a moment and then extended her hands to define a length of about six inches. "Oh, about this size."

Mr. Edwards laughed. "No, I mean do you need a flat-bladed one or a Phillips—you know, the kind with a cross on the tip?"

"Oh." Ann thought back to the rusty screwdriver she had taken out of the hangar. She remembered feeling the rusty tip with her finger. "Flat blade," Ann said confidently.

"Okay. So you need a flat blade about six inches long. How big of a head do you need?"

"I'm not sure," Ann replied.

"No problem. Here, let me show you what we have." Mr. Edwards opened a display case and retrieved several flat-bladed screwdrivers for Ann to inspect. The length of each was about six inches long, but the width and thickness of the blades varied.

Ann picked up each of them and tried to compare them with her memory of the screwdriver she had taken from Jack's hangar. She carefully felt the tip of each screwdriver until she found one that appeared to have the correct width. "This one. How much does it cost?"

"That's ninety-nine cents—plus four cents tax, of course, for a total of one dollar and three cents."

Ann plopped her coin sock on the counter and counted out the change to the apparent amusement of Mr. Edwards. She handed the correct amount in coins to him and picked up the screwdriver from the counter.

"Thank you, Mr. Edwards."

"Thank you, Ann. Say hello to your mother for me."

Ann ran outside to her bike and put the screwdriver in the basket. She pedaled home and took the screwdriver up to her bedroom. Rummaging through her closet, she found a small box that was big enough for the screwdriver and some leftover wrapping tissue and ribbon that she was saving for next Christmas. Ann put the screwdriver in the box and carefully wrapped the box in the tissue paper. She looped the thin red ribbon around the box and tied it in a bow. Ann sat back for a moment and admired her wrapping job before taking the wrapped box and running back down the stairs and out the door. Once again, she was careful to catch the screen door and close it quietly behind her.

Ann jumped on her bike and made her way back out to Jack's. As she approached the hangar, she could see the crop-dusting plane sitting out front. Jack's truck was parked beside the hangar. He was there. For a moment she hesitated, but she kept pedaling and made her way along the gravel road to the hangar. Her hands were trembling as she took the box out of the basket and carefully, quietly leaned her bike against the wall so that it wouldn't fall. She was so nervous that her stomach was tied up in a knot, but she was determined to see things through.

Through the open side door, she could see that Jack was at the workbench, engrossed in some project. She stopped at the threshold and knocked as loud as she could on the doorjamb.

Jack looked up from his work and stared at her, saying nothing for a moment. He put down a tool he was holding in his hand and addressed her. "I told you not to come back here."

"Yes, sir. I just wanted to apologize again for touching the plane. I know I shouldn't have."

"It doesn't matter now. What's done is done. Now get out of here and leave me alone."

"I also wanted to give you this." Ann held out the box with both of her hands, trying her best not to tremble.

"I don't want anything from you. Just leave me alone."

Ann felt crushed and stared down at her shoes. She fumbled with the box in her hands, picking at the bow. "I also wanted to tell you that I lied."

"Lied about what?"

"I lied about my father being dead and about him being a war hero. He wasn't in the war, and he didn't save anyone. I don't even know where he is now. He left me and my mom and never came back. He promised to come back for me, but he never did."

Jack took a rag from his back pocket and wiped his hands. He got up from the stool and walked slowly over to the door. "Why would you lie about something like that, kid?"

"I don't know. I just got tired of everyone teasing me all the time about not having a dad. I didn't want to tell them that he didn't want me. I wanted to have a dad I could be proud of, not one that didn't even want to know me."

Ann could see that Jack was becoming uncomfortable. He kept wiping his hands with the rag even though there was nothing left to wipe off.

Jack cleared his throat. "Listen, kid. Whatever your dad did, I'm sure it wasn't because of you."

"Yes, sir. I know that now. It was still wrong of me to say he was a war hero. You were a real war hero, and so was your son Henry."

Jack looked momentarily taken aback. "What do you know about my son?"

"Wild Bill told me he was shot down at Midway. I didn't know anything about Midway, but I went to the library and read all about it. Henry was very brave to go on that mission. I know you miss him. I know you blame yourself for teaching him to fly, but he would have done it anyway, just like you did when you volunteered to fly in World War I. You and Henry are the real heroes, not my father."

Ann noticed tears in Jack's eyes, and he didn't speak for a few minutes. Finally, he cleared his throat several times and asked, "Where did you say you heard about all this?"

"Wild Bill told me. I also looked in the box that you keep in the cabinet. I saw the picture of Henry and his medals and his uniform."

"You did what?" Jack said with alarm.

"I didn't take anything. I promise. I just looked at it and then put everything back where I found it. I promise I didn't take anything, but I was wrong to touch your things. I'm sorry."

Jack stood silently. His eyes glazed over. "It's just that it is all that I have left of him—what's in that box, the uniform they sent me, and his plane. I gave him that watch and ring when he graduated from high school. He was wearing them when they found him." Tears were running down Jack's cheeks. "He was going to fly that Waco around the country, making a living giving rides. We fixed it up together to get ready for the trip."

Jack wiped his eyes on his sleeve. "Then the war broke out. I never got to tell him how proud I was of him. I covered that plane up the day I found out that he had died and haven't looked at it since, not once."

Ann bent down and placed the box on the floor of the hangar without looking up. She couldn't meet Jack's eyes. "Yes, sir."

Ann ran out of the hangar, grabbed her bike, and rode off down the dusty gravel road.

***

Jack made his way to the door and watched Ann ride away until the dust trail from her bike was dispersed by the wind. Going back inside the hangar, he looked down at the neatly wrapped box. He reached down, picked up the box, and walked back over to the workbench. He sat down on the stool and placed the box in front of him on the workbench. After several minutes of staring at the box, Jack slipped the ribbon off and removed the tissue wrapping paper. He reached inside the box and pulled out the shiny new screwdriver. A small tag was tied onto the metal shaft. Jack looked at the neat block printing on the tag: "I'm sorry."

Chapter 12

Sarah thought she was dreaming again. The clock on her nightstand indicated it was 5:32 a.m., and the telephone was ringing. It was no dream. The telephone was really ringing. She got up, put on her robe, and shuffled down the stairs to the kitchen.

"Hello?" Sarah said in a groggy voice.

"Where's that kid of yours?"

"What? Jack, is that you? I thought you didn't want her there anymore."

"Tell her to get her behind over here. She's late, and I don't have all day to waste!"

"But—" Sarah heard a click on the line before she could get in another word. Jack had hung up on her again.

Sarah hurried upstairs to wake Ann. "Ann, get up. Jack called and wants you out at the hangar right away."

Ann sat up in her bed, rubbing the sleep out of her eyes.

"It was Jack. He said for you to get out to the hangar right now," Sarah repeated.

***

Finally registering what her mother was saying, Ann jumped out of bed and began searching for her clothes while her mother went back downstairs. She pulled on her shoes, which she hadn't bothered to untie when she kicked them off the night before. Half-hopping and running while fixing her shoes, she made her way down the stairs, where she found her mother holding the screen door wide open for her.

Ann raced out the door and jumped on her bike. As she took off, heading for Jack's as fast as she could, she heard her mother call after her, "Have fun!" A few minutes later, Ann turned the last bend in the dusty gravel road that brought the hangar into sight. She hit the brakes hard and skidded to a stop. There was a plane sitting out front, but it wasn't Jack's crop-dusting plane. It was the little yellow Cub. Ann continued down to the hangar, resting her bike up against the wall in the usual place. She managed to stop herself from just running through the open side door. Instead, she took a deep breath, walked calmly over to the side door, and knocked on the jamb. Jack was outside the open front hangar door, standing by the Cub, and didn't hear the knock. Ann gingerly stepped inside and made her way to the threshold of the large front door.

"You wanted to see me, sir?"

"Sneaking up on me again, are you?"

"No, sir."

Jack eyed her up and down. Then he looked at his watch. "Took your good time getting here, didn't you?"

"Sorry, sir."

"So you want to fly, do you?" Jack questioned.

Ann nodded her head.

"Are you going to take this seriously? No fooling around? No games?"

"Yes, sir."

"That's what they all say," Jack huffed. "First time I see you aren't paying attention and you're just wasting my time, we are done. Do you understand me?"

"Yes, sir."

"All right then. What's the first thing we do before we fly?"

"Preflight inspection."

"That's right." Jack nodded approvingly. "Come on."

Jack took her around the Cub and showed her how to open the cowling and check the oil, how to drain fuel to check for water contamination, and how to inspect the flight control surfaces and the propeller. The plane was different from the crop duster, but the process was very similar to what Jack had shown her when he first explained the preflight inspection to her. The one big difference was that they didn't have to rotate the propeller before starting the engine. Jack explained to her that the engine in the Cub was arranged with the cylinders in a horizontal configuration, which didn't cause oil to pool in any one cylinder like in the radial engine. As a result, it wasn't necessary to pull the prop through before starting the engine.

"Get in," Jack said, pointing to the front seat.

Ann jumped into the front seat, and Jack showed her how to fasten the shoulder harness and seat belt around her. He then explained the operation of the controls and the instruments, starting by pointing to a lever on the left side of the cockpit.

"That's the throttle, like the gas pedal in a car. Below that you see another knob on the side of the cockpit wall. That's the trim knob. You use that to adjust the trim and relieve pressure on the control stick. I'll show you how that works when we get in the air."

Jack pointed to the control stick protruding between Ann's legs. "Move the control stick left or right to control the ailerons and back and forth to control the elevator. The pedals down there control the rudder."

Ann moved the stick as instructed by Jack and watched the corresponding movement of the control surfaces. "What about brakes?" Ann asked. "How do you stop?"

"See those little small short pedals on the floor in front of the rudder pedals?"

Ann looked down. She had noticed them before and had even pressed them once or twice when she snuck into the plane, but she hadn't been able to tell what they were since they had caused no apparent movement of the control surfaces.

"Those are heel brake pedals. You slide the heel of your foot onto them and press. But in a small tail dragger like this one, you hardly ever touch the brakes, especially when you roll out after landing. It's too easy for you to hit the brakes hard and nose over or lose control. You just let the plane roll to a stop instead of using the brakes."

"So I never use them?"

"In windy conditions you might need them on the ground to help steer the plane. If you hold the right brake, the plane will swing to the right, and if you hold the left brake, the plane will swing to the left. Using the brakes to steer is called differential braking."

Ann nodded her head. It was all beginning to sound a lot more complicated than she had initially thought.

Jack pointed to the instrument panel next. "That's your airspeed indicator. It tells you how fast you are going. That's the altimeter, which shows your altitude. The tachometer shows you how fast the engine is running in revolutions per minute. That's called rpm. Over there is your turn coordinator."

Ann looked at the instruments pointed out by Jack. The airspeed indicator was simple enough to read. It was a round gauge with a single needle that pointed to numbers located around the gauge, just like a speedometer in a car. The tachometer was similar to the airspeed indicator, having just one needle pointing to numbers that indicated rpm. The altimeter, however, had two needles like hands on a clock. Ann wasn't sure how she could determine the altitude from the position of the needles. "Why does it have two needles?" she asked.

"The larger one shows your altitude in hundreds of feet, and the smaller one shows it in thousands of feet. It works like a clock, with the big needle acting like the minute hand and the little needle acting like the hour hand. One complete revolution of the big needle around is a thousand feet, so when the big needle goes around once and comes back up to the top, the little needle moves to the number one, indicating a thousand feet. Got it?"

Ann looked at the altimeter again. It had numbers around it just like a clock, except that the numbers went from zero to nine around the face instead of twelve to eleven like a clock. Ann nodded her head.

"Okay. Then if the little needle is on the one, and the big needle is on the three, what is your altitude?" Jack asked.

Ann thought about it for a moment before answering. "One thousand three hundred … thirteen hundred feet."

"That's right," Jack replied, as if surprised that she had gotten the correct answer.

Still looking at the altimeter, Ann noticed that the little hand was pointing straight up, but the large needle was between the zero and the number one. "Why aren't both needles on zero if we are on the ground?"

"Because the altimeter is set to indicate your altitude above sea level. Here in Indiantown, the airfield is about forty feet above sea level, so the altimeter is showing forty feet. We'll talk more about how that works and how you adjust it later."

Ann nodded again. "What is the turn coordinator for?"

"An airplane turns by changing the roll axis of the wings and banking." Jack demonstrated by holding his hand out flat and tilting it left and right. "But when you bank, you also have to control where the nose is pointing—that's yaw."

"You use the rudder for that, right?" Ann said, interrupting.

Jack, once again looking surprised, replied, "That's right. You didn't forget what I told you, did you?"

"No, sir. I remember everything you told me about flying."

"Hmm … we'll see about that when you're in the air. Anyway, when you turn, you have to use both the ailerons and the rudder in a coordinated manner. That ball in the glass tube tells you if the turn is coordinated. If the ball is to the left of center, you push the left rudder, and if it is right of center, the right rudder. Just think of it this way, and you won't get confused: you always step on the ball."

Ann looked at the turn coordinator. It contained a small, slightly curved, horizontal glass tube with a little black ball inside of it. The ball was currently sitting right in the middle of the tube since the plane was level on the ground.

Jack then handed her a small card with a printed list of instructions. He explained to her that the card contained a checklist of items that she was to perform before starting the engine and before taking off. He climbed into the backseat of the plane and had her run through the list of items on the checklist one at a time.

"Are you ready?" Jack asked.

Ann was both nervous and excited. "Yes, sir, but aren't we going to wear helmets with earphones like I did in Joe's plane?"

"Nah, you don't need no darn intercom," Jack replied in a disgusted voice.

"Well, then how will we talk to each other?" Ann asked.

"You don't need to be doing any talking. I'll do the talking, and you do the listening. Don't worry, you'll hear me over the engine noise. Are you ready now?"

"Yes, sir!" Ann replied enthusiastically.

"Okay then. Before you hit the starter button, you yell 'clear' to make sure everyone around knows that you are starting up the engine. You do it whether or not anyone is around so it becomes habit. Understand?"

Ann yelled out the window at the top of her lungs, "Clear!" She turned in Jack's direction. "How was that?"

"I'm sure they heard that two states over. Hit the starter, and remember I will be on the controls with you. I have dual controls in the backseat. If I say 'my airplane,' that means you let go of the stick and take your feet off the pedals immediately. Got it?"

"Yes, sir."

Ann hit the starter button as Jack had instructed her. The starter made a grinding sound, and the propeller began to turn. Suddenly, the engine kicked to life and roared.

"Throttle back, throttle back!" Jack shouted into her ear.

Ann was so excited that she had already forgotten where the throttle lever was located. Just when she remembered and was about to reach for it, she saw the lever slide backward, and the engine noise died down. Jack had already pulled the throttle back from the rear seat.

"When I tell you to do something, you do it without delay," Jack said in a stern voice.

"Yes, sir."

"Okay. I want you to taxi out to the end of the runway. There's no wind today, so just keep the control stick back as far as it will go. Later I'll show you how to taxi when you have to deal with the wind. You have to steer with the rudder when you are on the ground. The ailerons won't help, so moving the stick left and right isn't going to do you any good. Use your feet to steer on the ground. Okay, give it some gas."

Ann gingerly advanced the throttle. The engine noise grew louder, and the propeller spun faster. Suddenly, the plane began to roll forward and pick up speed. Ann instinctively pulled back on the throttle lever, and the plane slowed. She was excited but also nervous and anxious.

"Keep it at the pace of a slow walk," Jack said. As the plane rolled slowly forward, Jack shouted, "S turns! S turns!"

Ann realized that Jack wanted her to turn the plane back and forth as she had seen him do a hundred times. Otherwise, she wouldn't be able to see what was in front of her. Ann jerked the control stick to the right without thinking. The plane continued moving straight forward. She then jerked the control stick to the left, but the plane kept going straight. Her mind had gone blank, and she couldn't figure out what she was doing wrong.

"My airplane!" Jack yelled.

Ann immediately let go of the control stick and pulled her feet off the rudder pedals. Jack pulled the throttle back, and the plane rolled gently to a stop.

"What did I just tell you?"

"Uh ..." Ann stumbled to find the right answer.

"You steer on the ground with your feet. Moving that control stick isn't going to do you any good. This isn't a car or a bike. You don't steer on the ground with your hands. Now do it again. Your airplane. Repeat it back to me."

Ann tried to remember Jack's entire commentary from the beginning. "You steer on the ground ..."

"No, no, no. Don't repeat back the whole thing. When I say 'your airplane,' you acknowledge by saying 'my airplane.' That way we are both clear on who's got control of the airplane. Same thing when I say 'my airplane.' You acknowledge by saying 'your airplane.'"

Ann felt frustration rising within her, but she didn't want to let it show to Jack. She turned her head in his direction the best she could while strapped into her seat. "Well, you never told me that!" she shouted in the calmest voice she could muster over the engine noise.

Jack shouted back in an all-knowing, matter-of-fact manner, "Well, I'm telling you now! Get going." Jack pointed forward.

Ann turned around and pushed the throttle forward again while holding the stick steady and straight back. The plane began rolling forward. Ann pushed hard on the right rudder pedal, and the plane swerved to the right. She immediately recognized that she had pushed too hard and compensated by pushing hard on the left pedal. The plane stopped swerving right and instead swerved left. She had overcompensated once again.

"Are you trying to make me sick back here?" Jack yelled from the backseat.

Ann ignored his comment and focused on trying to get just the right amount of pressure on the rudder pedals to gently turn the plane from side to side. Jack had her practice taxiing up and down the runway several times. It didn't take long before she was performing smooth S turns, allowing her to see in front of the airplane as they progressed forward.

"Okay. Take it down to the end and line up with the center of the runway."

Ann was already sweating profusely, and they hadn't even gotten off the ground. She managed to line the plane up with the center of the runway as Jack had instructed.

"Don't we need to close the door?" Ann asked.

"Why? You worried about falling out? Leave it open so we can get some air."

Ann nodded her acknowledgement even though it seemed a little strange to leave the side of the plane wide open. She tugged her seat belt a bit tighter.

"Okay. I want you to give it full throttle and keep the stick back. When we get enough speed, just release some pressure on the stick, and the plane will fly itself off the runway. You just have to keep it straight using the rudder."

"How much speed? Should I watch the airspeed indicator?" Ann asked nervously.

"Don't worry about that for now. The plane will know when it is ready to fly. It's smarter than you. You just keep it straight. Use your peripheral vision."

Ann took a deep breath and pushed the throttle full forward. The engine roared to life, and the plane began to build up speed. Ann couldn't see anything in front of her, but she could sense the plane was pulling to the left, so she pressed on the right rudder. Again, she had pushed too hard, and the plane began swinging right.

"Too much, too much!" Jack called out immediately from the back.

Ann let some pressure off the rudder pedal. The plane straightened out and continued to build speed.

"Ease off the stick a bit," Jack shouted.

Ann glanced down and realized she had a death grip on the stick. She was holding it so hard her knuckles had gone white. Her heart was pounding so hard she thought it would pop out of her chest. She relaxed her grip on the stick and eased off on the pressure. Suddenly, the plane was airborne and climbing rapidly away from the grass.

"Keep it steady until you reach fifteen hundred feet."

She looked down at the altimeter. The large needle was rapidly moving around the face.

Five hundred.

Six hundred.

Seven hundred.

Eight hundred.

Nine hundred.

The numbers kept clicking off as the large needle passed the zero mark, and finally, she noted that the small needle was pointing at 1. They were at one thousand feet. The large needle continued its rotation. When it passed the number 4, she heard Jack yell from the back, "Okay, ease the throttle back until the engine rpm is at nineteen hundred!"

Ann pulled back on the throttle. She noticed that the nose of the airplane started to drop. The rate of climb slowed. When the rpm reached

1900, the plane had leveled out, and she could just see forward over the engine cowling. The altimeter read 1550 feet.

"Not bad. Not bad." She felt a pat on her shoulder as Jack congratulated her. Ann felt a sense of relief.

"Keep the plane level," Jack said. "Tell me what you feel."

Ann noticed that she had to keep some back pressure on the stick to keep the nose from dropping. "I have to hold the stick back to keep the nose up," Ann shouted back over the engine noise.

"Okay. That means you need to trim the nose up. Pull back on the trim knob very gently until you feel the pressure relieved in the stick."

Ann mistakenly pulled back on the throttle instead of the trim knob. The engine died, and the nose dropped.

Jack reacted immediately, pushing the throttle forward again while simultaneously giving Ann a rap on the back of her head with a wooden ruler he had brought along unbeknownst to Ann.

"Ouch!" Ann yelled.

"I said the trim knob, not the throttle!"

"Okay, okay. I'm sorry!" Ann yelled, again competing with the engine noise.

"Don't be sorry. Sorry doesn't help. Trim the airplane!" Jack replied.

Ann kept her right hand on the stick and used her left hand to pull the trim knob back. She felt the pressure release in the stick. She didn't have to pull the stick back to keep the nose up anymore.

"Did you feel it?" Jack asked.

"Yes. I don't need to hold the stick with as much pressure."

"Okay then. Take your hands and feet off the controls."

"What? Are you going to fly it?" Ann shouted in a concerned voice.

"Do what I tell you!" Jack shouted back. Ann felt a rap on the back of her head again.

"Ouch!" she cried out. "Hey, stop that!"

"Do what I tell you. Take your hands and feet off the controls," Jack repeated.

Ann did as Jack instructed and nervously removed her hands from the control stick and her feet from the rudder pedals. To her surprise, the plane continued to fly straight and level without her help.

"If you trim the plane properly, it will fly by itself. Good job," Jack yelled as he patted her on the shoulder.

A smile grew across Ann's face at the sign of Jack's approval.

"Now for some turns. Take the controls again, and I want you to make a turn to the left."

Ann took the control stick and moved it gently to the left. The left wing began to dip, and the right wing rose upward. The nose of the plane was pointing to the right, though, instead of to the left. Ann pushed the stick farther to the left, but the nose kept pointing toward the right.

"Center the ball! Center the ball!" Jack yelled, giving her another rap on the head.

Ann looked at the turn coordinator. The little black ball had rolled almost all the way to the left in the glass tube. She remembered Jack's reminder to step on the ball and pushed hard on the left rudder.

"Too much. Can't you feel that in the seat of your pants? Feel the airplane. Feel the airplane," Jack coached.

Once again, she had overcompensated. She eased off the left rudder until the ball was in the center of the tube and they were in a coordinated left turn.

"Okay. Level it back out."

Ann pushed the control stick slightly to the right. The right wing came down, and the left wing came up. She centered the control stick and eased off the rudder as the wings came level.

"I told you—you have to use the rudder and stick when making a turn. You weren't coordinated. Lead with the rudder. Do it again, this time to the right."

Jack continued to drill her, having her practice left and right turns and showing her how to climb and descend. She was getting tired, but she didn't want to tell Jack and have the lesson come to an end. It was Jack who finally called it a day.

"Okay, kid. You've had enough for one day, and I have work to do. You did well for your first time out."

Ann was absolutely ecstatic. She knew that getting a compliment out of Jack, especially about flying, was more difficult than getting blood from a stone.

"Would you like to fly over your house on the way back?" Jack shouted into her ear.

Ann perked up at the idea. She hadn't even given this any thought during the lesson, when she was concentrating so hard on trying to follow Jack's instructions. She had become totally disoriented through all the maneuvers and had no idea which way it was back to town or the airfield. She nodded in agreement, and Jack pointed the way.

After flying for a few minutes, Ann could make out the town below them. The scene below reminded her of the miniature houses and buildings she had seen in a model train layout in the toy department of a Baltimore department store during Christmas. She was quickly able to identify her neighborhood with respect to the town square. Flying closer, she picked up her street and then finally her house. It was both exciting and strange to see it from the air. It looked so tiny.

"Can I circle?" Ann asked.

"Knock yourself out, kid."

Ann banked the plane left and began a wide circle as Jack had shown her. After the second time around, she saw a figure in the front yard of her house. It was her mother, looking up and waving to her with a dish towel. Ann waved back and straightened the plane out. She knew where the airfield was from here and pointed the plane in the right direction.

A minute later, she felt Jack tapping on her right shoulder. She turned to the right to see him pointing down through the open door panel at the town baseball field below. Ann marveled at the view. She had been so busy concentrating on flying that she hadn't bothered to look out the wide-open right side of the plane at the landscape passing beneath her. With the door and window open, it was almost like they were flying along with nothing supporting them. Now she knew why Jack liked flying with the door open.

Ann noticed that Jack was making a circling motion with his finger. Ann banked the plane to the right this time and circled the ball field.

***

Tommy was the first one to see Ann through the open right side of the plane as she circled no more than five hundred feet above them.

"Look! It's her!" Tommy yelled from right field as he pointed up toward the sky.

The boys stopped playing to watch the plane circle the field.

Joey just stared up in disbelief from the batter's box and said nothing.

Billy took off his glove, threw it on the ground, and kicked it all the way to second base from the pitcher's mound while cursing under his breath.

***

Ann didn't care about the boys' reactions. The engine hummed in a melodic tone. A warm breeze brushed across her cheeks from the open door. She was flying like a bird, with nothing but fabric holding her aloft, and she never wanted to come down.

About the Author

M arc Rossi is a West Palm Beach attorney. When he is not practicing law, Marc can be found flying above the beaches of southern Florida in his red biplane. Flying on Fabric is his debut novel that he hopes will foster an interest in aviation among young people and encourage them to follow their dreams.

TRUE DIRECTIONS
An affiliate of Tarcher Perigee

OUR MISSION

Tarcher Perigee's mission has always been to publish
books that contain great ideas. Why? Because:

GREAT LIVES BEGIN WITH GREAT IDEAS

At Tarcher Perigee, we recognize that many talented authors, speakers,
educators, and thought-leaders share this mission and deserve to be published –
many more than Tarcher Perigee can reasonably publish ourselves. True
Directions is ideal for authors and books that increase awareness, raise
consciousness, and inspire others to live their ideals and passions.

Like Tarcher Perigee, True Directions books are designed to do three things:
inspire, inform, and motivate.

Thus, True Directions is an ideal way for these important voices to
bring their messages of hope, healing, and help to the world.

Every book published by True Directions– whether it is non-fiction, memoir,
novel, poetry or children's book – continues Tarcher Perigee's mission to publish
works that bring positive change in the world. We invite you to join our mission.

For more information, see the True Directions website:

www.iUniverse.com/TrueDirections/SignUp

Be a part of Tarcher Perigee's community to bring positive change in this
world! See exclusive author videos, discover new and exciting books, learn
about upcoming events, connect with author blogs and websites, and more!
www.tarcherbooks.com

TRUE DIRECTIONS
AN AFFILIATE OF TARCHER PERIGEE